Thanks,
Stephen Kushman

WALL STREET'S CURSE

STEPHEN KUSHMAN

Copyright © 2010 by Stephen Kushman

ISBN 978-0-7414-6261-9

Printed in the United States of America

Published October 2012

INFINITY PUBLISHING
1094 New DeHaven Street, Suite 100
West Conshohocken, PA 19428-2713
Toll-free (877) BUY BOOK
Local Phone (610) 941-9999
Fax (610) 941-9959
Info@buybooksontheweb.com
www.buybooksontheweb.com

WALL STREET'S CURSE

Seven dysfunctional investors, all neighbors, combine their love of beer and a fascination with the stock market to form an investment club.

One night a month, intoxicated, the members of Futures Investment Club (F.I.C.) attempt the impossible – select high performance stocks.

And outsider attending F.I.C's monthly meetings, observing the members interact, would swear they were in a bar named Cheers, not a financial meeting.

Marginally organized, with no sense of direction, these ordinary investors initially select some winners, but anyone knowledgeable about investment clubs knows certain clubs are doomed from the start. Investing is serious business!

After several years of failure, F.I.C's broker recommends the club disband. The President of F.I.C, who hated being president, agrees and sets up the final meeting.

The meeting never happens, because the President of F.I.C is called into a private meeting with the Chief Financial Officer of the firm and is offered a deal no intelligent investor could fathom or refuse. The members of F.I.C elect to continue and are lucratively rewarded for successfully being unsuccessful. Why?

Economic experts around the world are trying to understand the strange movements of the market, especially blue chip stocks. What is driving the market to rise to record territory and suddenly crash? There're worried about the markets effect on the economy. What is triggering the collapse on Wall Street?

Imagine if the Federal Government knew of seven incompetent investors manipulating the economy by accurately predicting a market crash or rally.

The market is always about what's going to happen – timing is everything.

Look out Wall Street, you're about to be CURSED!

Prologue

The Election

The meeting started at six o'clock in Gary Glenn's air conditioned living room. The cold beers in frosted glasses quenched the thirsty members of F.I.C. (Futures Investment Club) He was voting for Mike Chitkowski, everyone else cast their secret vote for him – lucky him.

Mike Chitkowski wanted the presidency, but at the last minute refused the members discount offer of $50 to buy their votes.

Every member tested for the position by serving a one year term. Unfortunately, Trevor Goodman was a born leader; he knew he was going to win.

As soon as the vote count confirmed his victory, Trevor Goodman resigns, as he said he would.

"Unacceptable," declared the members of F.I.C., who remind the new president of F.I.C's Constitution, which states he must accept the position or risk expulsion.

Not to worry, the Constitution, like the By-Laws and every thing else the club was supposed to have in place, was never completed, and Trevor Goodman knew the secretary wouldn't be able to locate the rough draft, since he always lost or misplaced important paper work.

He'll resign several times before completing his "For Life" tenure.

The cell phone rings and the secretary of F.I.C cuts off any further discussions by saying, "The meeting is over, my wife is on her way home. Does everyone remember the date for next month's meeting?" Everyone nods his head.

The members of F.I.C leave a case of empty beer cans for Gary Glenn to clean up and walk home.

PART 1.

THE MEMBERS OF F.I.C.

Susan recognized Trevor Goodman immediately as she entered the package store. It took a few minutes of conversation before he realized one of the neighborhood kids has grown into a mature attractive brunette – just like her mother.

"You haven't changed" commented the young female. He was just another father then, now she's looking at a handsome married man.

"You have!" exclaimed Trevor Goodman.

"It's been eleven years since we moved to N.Y., how's your family doing?"

"Fine thanks. How are mom and dad doing?"

"They split up, but are happy and still friends." She notices his left hand, no wedding ring.

"Wow. I never thought they would separate. Are you visiting?"

"No. I just moved back due to a great job opportunity at Diverse Investment's Brokerage Firm."

"That's interesting, I just got elected President of an investment club."

The letter came in the mail, no phone call. The envelope had a return address of Diverse Investment's Brokerage Services, Main St., Unionville, Connecticut. The envelope was outlined in gold leaf trim with a dollar sign stamped on the back. Each member of F.I.C. opened the letter and read the message.

Dear F.I.C. Members,

The new President of F.I.C. has reserved the conference room at Diverse Investment's for your Sept 9, 1983 meeting. Please arrive at 7pm. Attendance is mandatory!

Sincerely Yours,
Susan Weber

The initial reaction of each member was the same; shock, disbelief, and laughter. They never thought the President would react this way. He was upset and made it clear – he didn't want the position. Now he's directing his anger at them again, dealing with the problem the only way he can.

"Did you receive the letter yet?" asks Gary Glenn.

"Came in yesterday," responds Jim O'Sullivan. "I think he's out done himself this time."

"So you think it's a joke?"

"Do I think it's a joke? Of course I do. It's his way of directing his anger at us for electing him president. Remember the last time he was ticked off at us he said "I don't get mad, I get even.""

"Your right, he got us good – still there's a Diverse Investment's brokerage office in town. I'm going to call Mike and have him check with the brokerage firm."

"It's a joke, there's no Susan Weber," says Jim O'Sullivan with assurance.

Mike Chitkowski calls the number and leaves a message on her answering machine. A couple of days later, Susan Weber returns his call.

After hearing Susan's sexy voice, the excited Mike Chitkowski calls every F.I.C. member to confirm there's a Susan Weber or someone claiming to be her.

They all agree to go along with the prank.

A second letter from Diverse Investment's brokerage firm arrives, containing forms each member must sign. They sign the forms - let the master prankster have his fun.

The first F.I.C. meeting under the direction of its new president is just a half hour away. The two cars, each carrying three members, arrived at the brokerage firm within seconds of each other. Waiting in the parking lot is the only walker, Steve Culcarta, who co-owns an auto body shop two blocks down from the brokerage office. After greeting one another, they walk towards the historic building's main entrance illuminated by special lighting, very impressive. Entering the lobby, the members are greeted by a large woman sitting behind a desk wearing ear phones and a small microphone wrapped around her face.

"Good evening, welcome to Diverse Investment's. How can I help you gentleman?"

Trevor Goodman steps forward to answer, "Were here for a seven o'clock meeting with Susan Weber."

The receptionist, speaking into her microphone, informs Susan a group of gentlemen have arrived for a seven o'clock meeting, should she direct them to the conference room?

"Susan will be right with you. Please ascend the stairs, bear right and the conference room is at the end of the corridor." She's staring at the President who is holding a case of beer with a shopping bag filled with snacks resting on top. "Excuse me sir, are you bringing in food and drinks?"

Trevor Goodman answers, "Yes, Susan said it was o.k."

"Hold on a second. Ms. Weber, it seems the gentlemen have brought drinks and food with them. By drinks I mean beer. I don't think that's allowed." A long pause, then the receptionist, in a shocked voice, says its o.k. with Susan.

Looking like tourists walking through a museum, they look left and right, checking out every office as they proceed down the main corridor to the conference room.

In the plush conference room, a large chandelier hanging from the ceiling immediately catches each members attention. Then, each pair of eyes followed along the thick circular oak conference table with its matching armed chairs over to two massive windows, which allowed investors sitting around the table a view of the center of town.

The President places the case of beer on one of the huge window sills, restricting the view.

Landscape paintings of Unionville meadows, rivers, and valleys hung on the walls creating a calm, peaceful mood. A sense of wealth radiated off the textured wall paper down past the chair rails to a well padded dark blue carpet with diamond shaped emblems interwoven precisely in the direction of the carpets weave. Cleverly hidden away in fake cabinets, ready to be used at a moments notice by conference room guests, were computers, projectors, a white board, T.V., phone, and VCR.

The beer cans were opened and they attacked the snacks while strategically selecting a chair to sit in. Mike Chitkowski sat to the right of the President, his right hand man. To the left of the President, going clockwise around the table, dressed in shirt and tie, sits Gary Glenn. To his left sits Jim O'Sullivan a licensed electrician fully clad in the company overalls with cigars sticking out of his pocket. Next sat Steve Culcarta holding onto a large red plastic cup filled with vodka and soda while clothed in an S& D auto body uniform. In-between Steve Culcarta and Benny Benson sits Mario Bossi, a mason by trade, sitting with his huge forearms crossed, waiting impatiently for a bag of snacks to come his way. The last seat was occupied by Benny Benson, a small framed individual wearing a polo shirt with the name of his fitness club stitched on his pocket.

Starting with tonight's meeting and for reasons still a mystery to the President of F.I.C, yet probably understood by the famous Dr.Pavlov and his dogs, the members will forever sit in the same seats. Unexplainable still, is the reasoning behind the fact that when a member was absent, no one else sat in that vacant seat. Attendance was taken by simply looking at the empty seats people assigned to themselves to see who was missing. Stranger still, if someone accidentally sat in another member's seat, all hell would break out trying to figure out what that person was thinking about.

The members are now waiting for Susan to appear.

Susan is anxious, but ready to meet the members of F.I.C. She's grateful the CFO of the firm allowed her access to the other three investment club's meetings to observe and take notes. She is going to impress the president and the members of F.I.C with her organization and preparation, not to mention her leather outfit. Susan heads for the noisy conference room at the other end of the main corridor.

In walks Demi Moore's twin sister wearing a hot leather outfit. The members of F.I.C are frozen in place, staring at Susan in complete silence. They never heard a word the President was saying, since they were all staring at Susan's body tightly wrapped in a leather outfit.

Trevor Goodman was attempting to formally introduce Susan by stating he's known Susan ever since she was a little girl living in the neighborhood, and for reasons he feels was meant to be, had a chance meeting with her three weeks ago.

Susan always enjoyed seeing the reactions of men to her appearance; she had no problem flaunting her attributes – but her initial reaction to seeing the members of F.I.C face to face was shocking.

Benny Benson and Mario Bossi, the smallest and largest members, were standing together looking out the conference windows while holding a beer in their hands when both men turned to check out the female guest of honor. Gary Glenn and Jim O'Sullivan were sitting around the conference table. Gary Glenn's jaw dropped upon seeing Susan, exposing unchewed cashew nuts in his mouth, while Jim O'Sullivan was frozen in position with a cigar in one hand and a lit match in the other. Mike Chitkowski and Steve Culcarta, holding a beer in their hands, turned their heads away from discussing the famous wall paintings to focusing on Susan, quickly ending any artistic cultural emotions between them.

This wasn't what Susan expected. Based on her observations, the men should be wearing dress shirts, not uniforms, drinking freshly brewed coffee, not beer, and privately generating serious conversations about the market among themselves in a smoke free environment. She looks towards the president for an explanation...

Trevor Goodman quickly states, "Let me introduce you to the members of F.I.C."

The first member to be introduced by the President was Gary Glenn, who resembled the Cincinnati baseball player Pete Rose. "Gary is a world traveler, happily married with three children. He was elected secretary because no one else wanted the position. He'll be the only member in a shirt and tie, since he doesn't have time to change at home before the meetings. He sells Cannon cameras and copying machines in-between restaurant visits and golf matches. Gary, did you eat in an Italian restaurant today?"

"How did you know?"

"Because your shirt has food stains on it – looks a lot like pasta. Gary's favorite activity is eating. Did you bring last months minutes with you?"

"I told you I don't have time to do all that crap." Realizing what he just said, Gary looks at Susan while finishing his mouthful of cashew nuts, and apologizes. "You know I just had laser surgery on my eyes, causing eye irritation and tearing when reading or taking notes. Plus, I forgot my reading glasses last month, and Benny was supposed to take the minutes for me. As I said last month and I'm saying it again, we don't need to take minutes, nothing important is ever said. (Pause) I'm sorry, I had a terrible day at work, I didn't mean what I just said - I'm tired from traveling."

The President glances at Susan and decides to keep the introductions to just marital status, number of kids, and occupation.

Benny Benson, who looks and talks like Joe Pecsi, is standing behind the secretary, holding up an empty can of cashew nuts and asks, "Did you eat the whole freaking can of cashews by yourself?"

"I'm hungry, I didn't have supper!" snaps Gary Glenn.

The President tells Susan he brought a copy of last months meeting with him and tries to regain control.

"I like to discuss the amount of food at our meetings under new business. As a salesman, I attend many meetings all over the country and good food usually makes a good meeting. So, each member should consider the fact some members come directly to the meetings from work without eating supper. It's important that enough food be brought to the meetings," requests Gary Glenn.

"We can do that," says Trevor Goodman.

"Keep the rest of the snacks away from blimpy," wise cracked Benny Benson.

Michael Chitkowski, refocusing on Susan says, "You look gorgeous in leather. Are you married?"

Susan shakes her head, indicating a no answer.

Noticing Michael Chitkowski is starting to drool over Susan, Benny Benson tells her, "Please tell Mike, who just got divorced, you're not interested in dating computer geeks, because stupid is going to hit on you following the meeting."

Before the angry, red faced Mike Chitkowski could speak, the President quickly intercedes "This is Jim O'Sullivan. Jim is happily married with one child, and as you can see by the uniform, he's an electrician. He used to teach in an electrical shop at a vocational technical high school - but due to a physical confrontation with the principal – breaking his balls and nose - he ended up working for an electrical company owned by his best friend."

"Sorry to interrupt my introduction, does anyone want a cigar?"

Several members take a cigar from Jim O'Sullivan.

Susan is watching the conference room fill with cigar smoke. She doesn't remember authorizing beer drinking or smoking in the conference room. She is not happy.

Jim O'Sullivan asks Susan "How much money is this costing the President?"

"Excuse me?"

"Honey the joke is over, were not stupid." says Benny Benson.

"Speak for yourself" remarks Mike Chitkowski.

"What are they talking about?" a confused Susan is looking at the President for an explanation.

Mario Bossi adds, "You can relax and have a beer, you did good."

"The letter was clever and those forms you sent were pretty authentic, but we know what's going on," admits Steve Culcarta.

"So how much for the room, the outfit, and the fat receptionist?" asks Benny Benson.

Clearly agitated by the remarks, Susan demands an answer from the President, "What are they talking about?"

"I can explain. They think this is all a joke. I'm a practical joker, and they know if I'm mad, I'll go to any cost to get even with them. I don't want to be president "for life" and resigned already. They can't believe we meet and this whole event is real, so bare with me."

A voice inside Susan's head is saying "walk out" your dealing with children.

"Mario and Gary, you remember Bruce and Jenna Weber from Knoll wood road?"

"Of course we do," answers Gary Glenn.

"Susan is their daughter."

Mario and Gary are amazed.

"Holy shit, she does look like her mother," exclaims Mario.

Trevor Goodman needs to gain control "Guys, this is no joke. If you're forcing me to be president for life, then it's time to get serious, become a real investment club, not a men's club. You can go down the hallway and see Susan's office, or call anyone at the firm tomorrow to confirm she's our broker. Starting tonight, and with Susan's guidance, we're going to become the top investment club within this firm. So listen and pay attention, we're here for only an hour and a half. Susan has a lot to cover in a short time frame."

"I'm convinced this is no joke," says Gary Glenn, directing his response to everyone in the room.

"Me too" concludes Mario Bossi.

Trevor Goodman speaks, "Good, let me continue with the introductions."

Susan needs to stop the meeting. Looking directly at the President she speaks, "Stop the introductions, I don't think this is going to work. It's obvious I'm already in trouble by allowing you to drink and smoke in here. I spent a lot of time preparing for this meeting and took your word that you were serious investors. Please clean the place up and leave the windows open when you leave." She can't believe the mess the members made of the conference room in only a few minutes. Turning towards the members she says, "It was nice meeting all of you, good luck with your club." She walks out of the conference room.

Steve Culcarta turns towards the President and asks, "Why did you tell her we were serious investors?"

"I don't know why, maybe I thought we could become serious investors with her help. I'm going to apologize and hope she reconsiders"

"If Benny kept his mouth shut, she probably wouldn't have walked out" adds Mike Chitkowski.

Benny Benson snaps back, "She left because she saw the little pup tent rising in your pants."

Trevor Goodman proceeds down the corridor to Susan's office hoping the group won't come to blows for a few minutes while he's gone.

Susan was already on the phone calling the CFO (Chief Financial Officer) to apologize for allowing beer and smoking in the conference room. She explained how she walked out, and doesn't feel comfortable with assisting this group – their not serious investors as she was told – she doesn't want to be associated with them – there not like the other clubs. The CFO was about to respond when the President standing behind Susan listening to her apologize, grabs the phone away from Susan to speak to the CFO.

"My name is Trevor Goodman, the president of F.I.C. Susan shouldn't be reprimanded for what happened tonight, and it's my fault. I wasn't honest with your receptionist or Susan. They had no idea we would be drinking or smoking tonight. Please don't punish Susan for this misunderstanding."

The CFO remembers the name of the investment club and finds it ironic that the names were almost the same. The members of the Farmington Investment Club were a wild bunch of characters too. "Thank you for taking responsibility for tonight's misunderstanding, Susan is not in trouble. In fact I'm going to tell Susan to go back and restart the meeting. We'll discuss the drinking and smoking problem later."

Susan gets back on the phone and is told by the CFO to give it another try. He explains that this incident has happened before. The investment club you observed last month was worse than F.I.C when they started, so don't give up; you'll be fine, just make sure you cover everything he and she discussed.

Susan wondered out loud," How could anyone be worse than F.I.C?"

Upon returning to the conference room, Susan and the President observe the members huddled together around the conference table discussing Susan's exit.

Jim O'Sullivan speaks for the group. "We're willing to go half way, we'll get serious, won't smoke inside, but we're not giving up beer."

Susan can't believe this is happening.

The President wants to finish the introductions and asks, "Who hasn't been introduced yet?"

Four hands go up in the air, three holding onto a can of beer, and one holding a red plastic cup with a crushed car logo on the side.

"This is Benny Benson."

"Nice to meet you, I'm going to guess your measurements are 38 -24 -36, am I close?"

Susan really wants to leave, but glances at the President again.

"Benny isn't afraid to speak his mind, even if it angers people. He owns the fitness club on Desoto Drive. Benny's happily married with two children."

Susan visited the club last week to seek membership. She has second thoughts about joining.

Pointing to the back of the room "That's Mario Bossi, a mason by trade; he's happily married with two children." Mario Bossi sits his massive 6' 3", 250 lb. body on a chair next to the beer supporting window sill.

Trevor Goodman turns towards Mike Chitkowski to introduce him, but he's already standing in front of Susan, adjusting his wire rim glasses as he extends his hand to shake hers.

"If you ever need any help with computers, just give me a call."

"Mike is thinking about changing his name because so many people make fun of Shit - kowski." jabbed Benny Benson.

Susan was actually wondering if the name was spelled as it sounded.

"So he's decided on George instead of Mike."

Even Susan cracked a smile reacting to Benny's humor, everyone in the room laughs -except Mike.

"That's not funny!" Protested Mike Chitkowski - who looks a lot like the actor Paul Giamati.

The President continues "Mike is divorced, has a son, and is Unionville High School's computer coordinator."

Mike is the only member who hasn't taken his eyes off Susan since she entered the conference room, unless she looked at him. Scary, thought Susan.

The last member to be introduced is Steve Culcarta, who resembles the golf pro "The Shark" with his blond hair and famous smile.

"Steve Culcarta is the co-owner of S&D auto body around the corner. He's happily married with two children."

Susan is focusing on Steve's uniform shirt pocket which along with his name included a small bottle of vodka tucked inside – similar in size to airplane liquor bottles. Steve mentions the possibility of servicing Susan's car if she so needed.

With the introductions complete, the President turns the meeting over to Susan.

Her mind is wandering, thinking about her presentation, which she practiced over and over again; make it short and precise, explain the materials clearly and make it easy for everyone to understand. Then hope to answer questions presented to her by the members with professional ease.

Susan really wants to leave the room. She planned a power point presentation to coincide with the packet of materials handed to each member. This was designed to impress the members using the state of art technology hidden within the walls of the conference room, but she's afraid to turn off the lights, and put everyone to sleep. Plus she never planned a presentation around seven alcoholics - God knows how many beers they'll drink during the twenty minute presentation. Susan decides to quickly go through each page of the packet, get the hell out of there, and save the power point presentation for another investment club.

She stressed only what was on page two of the packet - the top five reasons why investment clubs fail. 1. Not organized 2. Low attendance 3. Personnel conflicts 4. Poor stock selections and 5. Member relocation.

With rapid speed, she finishes her explanation of the materials, asks if there are any questions, which there were none, and wishes the club well until we meet again next month.

"Not so fast honey. How much commission are you getting?" asks Benny Benson.

"We'll discuss that at the next meeting" answers Susan as if she would be at the next meeting, hopefully it will be someone else.

She ends the meeting by reminding everyone to select a stock to report on for next month's meeting and wishes everyone well. Susan isn't planning on seeing the members of F.I.C again.

The members of F.I.C. are dumbfounded. The new President is causing the members a lot of stress by changing the game plan. Becoming real investors isn't going to be easy.

Just when everyone is rising to leave, Trevor Goodman announces he's selecting Mike Chitkowski as the new treasurer of F.I.C.

"You can't do that without a vote" expresses Benny Benson who is the current treasurer.

"I will resign if my wishes are not fulfilled." Everyone laughs except Mike. No one takes the president's threat seriously.

Benny continues, "You're picking Mike because he thinks you're God and will never disagree with you about anything - plus you know he wanted to be president."

Mike is in shock but manages to look at Benny Benson before he acknowledges the president, "I would be honored to serve as your new treasurer and won't let you down."

"I think I'm going to puke!" says Benny Benson.

Everyone congratulates Mike, except Benny.

The new treasurer is assigned the responsibility of working on the Constitution, By-Laws, and tax forms for next months meeting. Benny Benson was right; the treasurer would do anything for the president, especially when it was the president and only the president who helped him through a messy divorce by taking care of his son until things settled down.

As the members leave the brokerage firm and head for their cars, Benny Benson calls everyone together to look at his cell phone pictures of Susan. "Check these three shots out," chuckled Benny. The pictures captured Susan bending over, one from the front and the other from the rear, plus a side view of her standing in front of the conference table. Looking at Mike Chitkowski, he offers copies of each picture to Mike for $10 dollars. Mike pays him the ten dollars – everyone laughs all the way to the cars.

TREVOR GOODMAN

The instant recognition, he was aware of the attention, but never used it to his advantage. Trevor Goodman considered himself an average looking guy. Not according to his buddies, who frequently pointed out which female was staring the longest.

His beautiful wife also reminded him of the attention he created, yet knew he would never cheat on her. Their relationship was solid, unbelievably tight – she never questioned his hatred of wearing jewelry, especially a wedding ring.

Physically fit, up early to exercise daily, he looked five years younger than his age. In his mid-thirties, happily married with two children, he felt blessed.

College degrees in General Science and Physical Education, allowed him to secure a teaching and coaching position in the City of Hartford, were he was born and raised.

A person who stayed away from confrontations, but wasn't afraid to fight when cornered, he won more battles then he lost, especially on the football field, were he excelled as a player.

A hard worker, who always held more then one job, he saved more cash then he spent. Making a decent living, spending time with the wife and kids, provided him with a comfortable life.

Once in a while, like relatives and friends, who knew the chances of winning in these areas were slim, he would purchase a lotto ticket, visit a casino, or bet on sporting events, with no luck. His wife, a nurse, who worked many hours, hated seeing hard earned money going down the drain, but allowed and accepted his minor gambling habits.

What intrigued him was the risk people took playing the stock market. Individual investors, like his neighbors, who constantly pressured him to play the market, because in the long run he'll make more money investing in Coke a Cola, McDonalds, and AT&T, then in a bank. Even his financial advisor suggested it was safe to dabble in the market, assuring the diversity of future retirement funds should include safe low risk investments in the stock market. Right now, his secure, safe retirement plan consisted of saving and credit union accounts, pensions, insurance policies, and social security.

Other people, his father in - law, brother, co-workers, parents, also said to get into the stock market. They claimed the risks were lower then the rewards. Everybody except him seemed to own stocks, but he couldn't afford buying hundreds of shares of stocks. Plus, wasn't playing the market gambling?

While entertaining the neighbors with a backyard cookout and consuming a few beers, an idea formulated in his head. Would they be interested in starting an investment club?

As an individual investor, the future will show, he made a wise decision to join forces with them.

Unfortunately, the entire country will suffer financially from their efforts.

Trevor Goodman only had a month to research the president's position, so he headed to the library to learn how to start an investment club, how to manage a club, and how to be successful in selecting stocks. He actually thought he might control the group by knowing additional facts regarding the functions of an investment club.

While in the library, he overhears two women discuss the "veggie burgers their husbands cooked on the grill." They claimed the burgers tasted better than regular hamburgers. He gets the name of the company and decides to present the stock at next month's meeting for consideration.

GARY GLENN

The oldest member of the investment club at thirty eight years old, Gary Glenn has a month to type and mail the minutes of the meeting to the members of F.I.C. In the past, he never did his job, and no one cared, but now things have changed. According to Susan, the minutes needed to be in everyone's hands before the next meeting. Bull shit! The only thing that he needed to do was bring the beer and lots of snacks, it was his turn, besides he saw the president taking notes.

The decision to purchase "ice beer" for next months meeting wasn't his idea, but a client's. His client told him ice beer contained a higher alcohol percentage than regular beer, yet cost about the same. How can that be?

After drinking four ice beers together and speaking in slurred speech patterns, Trevor Goodman, Jim O'Sullivan, and Gary Glenn proclaimed ice beer as the official beer of F.I.C. In fact, after several more ice beers, the president of F.I.C wanted to know who the genius was who told Gary about ice beer – "Lets invite the person to join the club and make him president."

A people person, perfect for sales, Gary Glenn could wine and dine you into buying anything. A smooth operator, he knew his trade and would rise up through the ranks within the company because of hard work and expertise in troubleshooting. He traveled the world, and loved all the restaurants he ate at the company's expense. A great golfer, he was tough to beat.

He was always on the golf course, which made him very knowledgeable about golf equipment. This area of expertise allowed him to hear about an IPO that was going to be offered by Club Golf Incorporated at $10 a share. He didn't know what an initial public offering was, but decides to offer Club Golf as a stock of choice at next months meeting. A decorated Vietnam veteran, he served two tours of duty.

Gary Glenn and Trevor Goodman are hunting buddies. They only hunt for pheasants. One memorable day of hunting was in October on state owned land in New Hartford, Ct.

Gary Glenn, a Dirty Harry fan, announced, as the two hunters were getting ready for the hunt, that he'll be using magnum shot gun shells today in honor of Clint Eastwood.

Gary never shot a pheasant while hunting with Trevor Goodman. Trevor had the quickest reaction time and was very accurate – causing Gary to basically carry his shotgun for exercise. It would have been to the Gary's advantage to carry hand grenades then a shotgun.

They started to hunt in an area covered with large fern plants and thick pricker bushes – areas even hunting dogs wouldn't run through. The first pheasant was flushed out of the bushes due to Gary accidentally stepping on it, as it sat hiding from the other hunters. The pheasant ran along the ground before it flew up about 15yards to the right side of Gary. Trevor Goodman couldn't shoot it because Gary was in the way – but Gary unloaded three magnum shots and missed. Trevor couldn't believe how fast it flew and how quick it landed.

Gary noticed the exact spot where it landed – "He's right next to the white birch tree," says an excited hunter. Using the birch tree as a marker, they surrounded the tree and moved slowly until the bird was flushed out for the second time. Again, the bird flies away from Trevor Goodman, angling towards the side of Gary Glenn who unloads 3 more magnum shots and misses. The pheasant was flying at supersonic speeds, but lands only about 10yds.from both hunters. "Did you see how big that bird is?" questions Gary Glenn. Trevor Goodman answers by telling Gary he saw the numbers 747 on its tail. "How could you miss that huge bird?"

Upset over missing again, Gary tells Trevor he saw the bird land next to a huge boulder out in a clearing. They can't believe the simplicity of relocating the bird. This time Trevor tells Gary to flush the bird from the other side, so he has a shot. The bird is flushed for the third time – both shoot three rounds off. Gary misses –but Trevor shoots the pheasant's legs off. The 747 is now flying without landing gear. The bird is the fastest pheasant they've ever encountered –but the dumbest – since it flies a short distance and lands again. Gary's shotgun barrel is smoking and red hot from firing magnum shells – if they miss the bird this time – he wants to take a break and cool down his shotgun. He tells Trevor that he saw the bird land next to a fence post. Trevor acknowledges Gary by stating the following: "To bad you can't shoot as well as you can see."

They surround the pheasant (fence post). Other hunters are starting to appear due to the sound of gun fire and their curiosity of seeing how many birds have been shot. With other hunters watching, they flush the bird up for the fourth time. They both miss the bird as it flies towards the other hunters who also shoot and miss. The bird has been shot at 16 times counting all the rounds and is still flying freely - without legs.

Gary needs to cool down his shotgun barrel, so they sit up high on a ridge over looking the area they just hunted while watching some hunting dogs flush out birds. As they are resting, Trevor hears something moving to his right along a wide path leading down the ridge. Both hunters look towards the noise and suddenly a pheasant – with very similar markings on it from the one they've been trying to shoot - appears. The pheasant is flapping its wings, as it sits in what appears to be a squirrel's nest up in a small tree next to the path, and turns his head towards Trevor Goodman and Gary Glenn as if to say – "not you guys again."

"Could it be his twin brother?" asks Gary.

They slowly pick up their shotguns and fire six more rounds of ammunition at the bird and miss, but another hunter also fires a round off sending the bird back towards Trevor and Gary who quickly identify the bird as the same legless pheasant as it flies over their heads. Gary can't believe the bird flies into a wood pile 20 yards down range. Gary and Trevor surround the wood pile and flush the bird up again. Trevor's gun jams as Gary unloads three magnum shots and hits the bird. As they try to find the bird, another hunter approaches them and asks what kind of shotgun shells are you using? I've never seen a bird blow apart like that before. Gary Glenn tells the hunter he's using magnum shells as feathers start to fall from the sky.

MICHAEL CHITKOWSKI

Mike Chitkowski was in his mid thirty's and took everything in life seriously – too seriously. Winning custody of his son and his house in the divorce settlement drastically changed his life. He just lost his mother and decided to take in his ailing father which eliminated any time for a social life. Mike's membership in F.I.C was going to allow him to socialize one night a month, make lots of money in stocks, drink lots of beer and maybe go on some road trips. It was an honor to be chosen treasurer and he did an excellent job.

His name appeared in the local paper after being selected teacher of the year – the first time a computer coordinator was honored by a school system in Connecticut. He alone reorganized the school's grading system, e-mail process, and substitute coverage through computerized programs developed within his computer classes.

Unfortunately while at the Connecticut State Capitol receiving his award, his car was stolen. Lucky for him he just installed a Lojack security system in his car. The car was quickly found without damage. Mike decides to offer Lojack stock for consideration at next months meeting.

He called the president to secretly discuss club rules, regulations, and consequences which he developed to maintain order. For example: poor attendance, failure to pay dues, and inappropriate language or remarks towards another member. He offered fines for each rule broken.

This created a dilemma for the president who didn't give a damn about who paid dues, attended meetings, or committed suicide, but he re-acted as any other leader would do in a crisis, he will resign if the rest of the members resist the treasurer's proposals.

Trevor Goodman was asked by Mike Chitkowski to babysit his Labrador retriever while he vacationed with his son. Trevor hated pets, and none were allowed in his house.

Trevor walked around the back of the house as instructed, up the deck to the bedroom atrium doors, opened them and noticed this huge dog lying quietly in a huge cage watching ESPN on T.V. The dog was so focused on the T.V. that he didn't know anyone was in the room.

As soon as Trevor Goodman went to reach for the leash hanging on the side of the cage, the dog goes berserk, starts jumping in the cage, whacking his tail against the side of the cage, and forces his head into the cage door, trying to get out. Trevor tries to carefully open the cage to attach the leash on him, when the huge powerful dog starts to escape the cage. Trevor had to wrestle the dog as if it were a rodeo bull. The dog takes off through the atrium doors just as the president attaches the leach, pulling Trevor Goodman down the steps of the deck, around the corner of the house, towards the street.

Trevor Goodman and the dog were headed towards a collision with a large tree standing in the front yard. Trevor holding the leash went to the right of the tree, while the dog went to the left, causing the leash to wrap around the tree, choking the dog. The dog's neck snapped backward, but he just runs around to Trevor's side and continues to pull the president up the street attacking anything that passed by – like people and other dogs. The dog would stop and smell other dog's crap – but he wouldn't crap. Trevor couldn't wait to get this crazy animal back in its cage. To get it back in the cage, he had to push the dog from behind, imitating a racehorse getting into the starting gate. He'll never do this again, he says to himself as he drives back home.

Back home, Trevor Goodman's children ask him how babysitting a dog went. Did you take him for a walk? Did you feed him? Feed him – ah shit – I forgot to feed him – says a ticked off president. He goes back to feed the dog, who thought he was getting out of the cage again, but Trevor Goodman feeds him through the cage, which causes the dog to crap. It takes him hours to clean up the mess.

As he entered the conference room, Mike Chitkowski noticed a packet lying on the table next to the phone. He was early for the meeting, and decides to walk down the corridor to Susan's office. While walking, he observes to his left and right as he passes each office, the same packet was on every broker's desk.

Susan quickly looks at her office clock and sees he's forty five minutes early.

"You're early, the meeting doesn't start until 7pm."

"I know. This was left in the conference room." Mike puts down a packet titled "Strategies for Success." He's standing behind Susan staring down her revealing low cut dress. "I thought you might be in your office getting things ready for tonight's meeting. Can I help you with anything?"

"Thanks, but I'm all set. She's certain he will be early for every meeting – she wants to tell him her office is off limits and please don't come in here unless your invited - but proceeds to inform Mike, "A young guy was in here yesterday trying to sell his computerized program to all the brokers. He left a copy with everyone, but no one was interested. He independently copyrighted and published this packet which also includes a CD rom. Why don't you look at the program and let me know what you think - you can use the computer in the other office."

"I think I will." Mike follows her suggestions.

The CD rom was placed in the office computer, and the treasurer brings up the material on the computer screen. The main program is designed for professional investors tracking the stock market on a daily basis. Using specific strategies, the computerized program will pop up "indicators" and "alerts" on the computer screen as each stock is selected by the investor, assisting the expert in his or her decision to buy or sell, creating a true sense of market movements. Unfortunately, a pass word must be entered for the computer to allow the investor into the main program. The treasurer shuts down the computer, and takes the card out of the inside cover of the packet, reading the name of Jim Frond, followed by his phone number.

Mike returns to Susan's office. "I'm going to give the guy a call. Listen would you like to go out to dinner, have a few drinks, a talk about the market?"

"Gee, that sounds exciting, but I'm not interested."

They walk back to the conference room together and set up the room for tonight's meeting which will start in about thirty minutes. The treasurer sits by the phone to call Jim Frond, while Susan goes back to her office. Since he's the first one to purchase Jim Frond's program, the price of the packet is discounted, allowing the treasurer to purchase the program at half price. Jim Frond will ship the packet out tomorrow.

The second member to arrive had a cold and began coughing and spitting up mucus while saying hello to the treasurer.

A disgusted treasurer says, "Why didn't you stay home? You look horrible. You're going to spread your germs to everyone else."

"Spread this!" says Benny Benson while pointing at his groin area seconds before Susan reenters the conference room.

Susan and Benny exchange greetings and in between sneezing, he says, "I hope you ignored Mike's advances tonight".

"Why don't you mind your own business?" requested Mike Chitkowski.

"Why don't you give it up stupid? She's never going to go out with you."

Susan gives Benny a surprised stare just as the next three members arrive together. Everyone says hello and unpacks the beer and snacks carried in by the secretary.

Susan tells the three some, "you arrived just in time", looking at Mike and Benny as they crack open their first ice beers.

The President doesn't waste anytime, while opening his first beer, he tells Gary Glenn to tell the joke he told in the car on the way over to the meeting.

"Why don't we wait for everyone else to arrive," suggested the secretary.

"Because you'll forget the joke by then," answers Jim O'Sullivan.

The secretary starts to tell the joke, when in come the last two members – Steve Culcarta and Mario Bossi. They exchange greetings, grab a beer, and Gary restarts his joke, while Benny Benson continues to cough, sneeze, and spit up mucus in the waste basket.

"Are you o.k.?" asks the President." You look like crap."

"I'll be fine, finish the joke," says Benny.

The members burst into laughter following the secretary's joke, followed by another joke from Jim O'Sullivan, topped off by an even funnier joke by Mario Bossi. The members were laughing so hard, tears were running down their faces.

The treasurer wants his turn at busting the guts of the other members by telling one more joke.

The joke is about a new Polish birth control method successfully used in Poland, "Did anyone hear the joke before?" asks Mike Chitkowski.

The members answer no, and Benny Benson is already laughing - at Mike.

He is doing the best he can with presenting the joke, and is about to stand up to deliver the punch line, which involves hand gestures, when out of the blue, Benny Benson stands up and finishes the joke, causing the treasurer to become very agitated. Everyone is laughing at Mike rather then the joke.

Benny asks the treasurer if he has any more old jokes, while coughing and laughing at the same time.

"I hate you!"responds a dejected treasurer as he tries to go after Benny.

The President quickly gets control of the meeting and asks everyone to settle down. He politely asks everyone to look over the materials in front of them. "Does anyone have any questions before we start?" There hasn't been a meeting when a member actually asked any questions, but the President continues to give them the opportunity.

In front of every member was a stack of papers placed on the conference table by the treasurer and Susan.

Susan is amazed Mike Chitkowski accomplished every task asked of him in one month's time. She compliments him on completing the tax forms, Constitution, and By-laws and notices the president was the only member looking over the materials.

The president asks the secretary to read the minutes of last weeks meeting.

With a mouth full of food, Gary Glenn answers he didn't have time to complete the minutes, but promises to have them ready for next month. Everybody laughs except Susan.

The president looks at Susan who quickly recommends the secretary stop eating and find a pencil and paper to start taking notes. She then requests the members create a method for buying or selling stocks by next month, eliminating future conflicts. Susan asks each member, starting with Gary Glenn, to report on stocks of interest.

Gary says he heard about an IPO being offered by Club Golf for $10 a share. He asks Susan to explain what an Initial Public Offering was to the members and she does, adding these offerings are very risky.

Jim O'Sullivan offers Sensory Alloy a new Connecticut company his brother heard about. The stock was selling for only $2/share and the future outlook for the company looked promising since a ten year contract was signed with a medical company to produce "metal stints", used in arteries of heart patients with blocked arteries.

The company also produced bi-metal products such as shower heads that automatically regulated (memorized) hot and cold water temperatures by a thermostat type metal that expands and contracts when stimulated by water pressure and temperature – automatically shutting down a shower if water was dangerously hot or freezing cold.

Samples of Sensory Alloy showerheads were brought to the meeting for people to take home and try. Only Benny Benson rushed to install this new product – because his wife insisted that he always had the water heater set to high in temperature. This beautiful looking device was going to solve his problem.

Steve Culcarta offers Gyrotest, a company interested in establishing emission centers through out the state of Ct. to test cars for emission violations. The price of Gyrotest was $5 a share. Eventually, the company will sell the testing equipment to gas stations, so cars can be tested at many sites, rather than one or two test centers.

It was only fitting that Mario Bossi, the gambler, heard about a stock called Industrial Gaming. A company that repairs and builds computer operated slot machines. He informs the club that this company was contracted by two of Ct. newest casinos to build and maintain their slot machines for the next ten years. (Also new casinos in Arizona and Montana). The company is located in Las Vegas and is the soul provider of gaming machines to the Mirage casino.

Mike Chitkowski offered Lojack, a security system for cars.

Red Alert, according to Benny Benson's wife (a school bus driver) is a company that created a safety devise that can alert a bus driver if a child is trying to walk in front or behind a school bus. By using laser technology and a metal type swing bar, children can safely be detected walking around school buses. The company also went into producing AED's (automated external defibrillators). AED's came in adult, child, and infant sizes, increasing the need by all schools, police, fire, and hospitals to purchase them.

Samples of "Veggie Burgers" were brought to the meeting by Trevor Goodman who strongly recommended F.I.C purchase 100 shares, "It's going to replace the hamburger, Mc Donald's is thinking about selling it." No one takes the samples home.

Susan wanted to discuss selecting small quantities of" Blue Chip" stocks and was about to talk when a vote count was requested by the president. She remained silent, wondering which stock would become the winner, but then recommended no one should vote for their own stock.

Three members of F.I.C voted for purchasing 100 shares of Club Golf at $10 a share and three members voted against. It was up to the president to break the tie. He votes for purchasing 100 shares. Three members call him a moron and threaten to kill him, while the other three cheer his choice.

Susan was instructed to call Trevor Goodman when the stock market opened the next morning to track the progress of the stock. At 9am the stock was up to $15 a share. At 9:01am some members of F.I.C start calling the president demanding he tell Susan to sell the stock. At 9:05am other members call to warn the president not to listen to the other jerks and wait until the market closes. Susan calls the president an hour before the closing bell to report that Club Golf is at $20 a share and asks - what do you want to do? Trevor Goodman tells her to sell the stock at $20 a share.

The President can't believe he just made a decision without consulting the members of F.I.C. What was going to happen if the stock continued to climb higher the next day? Wasn't everyone going to be happy with doubling their money? He could always resign if things went wrong – and to him that was a good option.

The phone starts ringing from all the members of F.I.C wanting to know what happen and why he didn't call them first before he decided to make a presidential decision. Everyone wants an emergency meeting tomorrow night to discuss Trevor Goodman's actions. The president knows he's going to resign at the meeting - so he agrees to schedule the meeting for 7pm tomorrow night at his house.

Club Golf opens the next morning at $15 a share. Late in the afternoon the stock drops down to $5 a share and remains at $5 a share for the rest of the week. The stock never came close to $10 a share for the next five months.

The president was now the greatest person on earth. Everyone started to think of ways F.I.C could celebrate its first big hit within the stock market. It was decided to take the profits ($3000) and road trip to a horse track betting pallor.

(Money spent =$3000 7 people x 12 races, plus food, drinks, and cigars. $400 / member in 5 hrs. Of entertainment. Total of $500 won at track – gone. Total amount of laughs – priceless. Designated driver – none. Lucky to make it home alive = 7 people.)

Gary Glenn, having just been awarded with a plaque titled – greatest member of F.I.C (Club Golf) – decides to inform the group of another stock he highly recommends purchasing called "Bioamerica". He has owed the stock for years as part of a mutual fund. He explains to everyone the stock's value is up $7 a share. "We need to jump on this right away because the last time it moved up it split shares 2 to 1." (Susan had to explain stock splits to the members.)

Bioamerica is a research company dealing with a vaccine for different forms of cancer. Its current price is $20 a share, a new 52 week high. The secretary persuades the members of F.I.C to purchase 100 shares of Bioamerica and forget about the other stocks offered last month.

The president was the only one to vote against the purchase of Bioamerica. He did this by admitting to all members he was upset the plaque "Greatest Member of F.I.C" was awarded to Gary Glenn only, and not to him, since he made the tough decision to go ahead with the purchase of Club Golf. This shocked the members of F.I.C.

The secretary of F.I.C calls the president at the end of the week – excited about "Biometric" climbing to $29 a share. Trevor Goodman – confused – asks Gary Glenn to repeat what he just said. The secretary again boosting about his choice of buying" Biometric" at this time, tells the president to call everyone to let them know another plaque is due since the purchase of "Biometric" is going to break another F.I.C record. The secretary says the whole market is up and Biometric is right up there with the top ten blue chip stocks.

The President now informs Gary that F.I.C purchased 100 shares of "Bioamerica" not "Biometric". Then adds, "How's Bioamerica doing?"

"Holy shit!" We bought "Bioamerica" instead of "Biometric." A confused secretary asks, "How the hell did that happen?"

Trevor Goodman answers; "Let me explain, you drank a lot of beer at my house. You were having trouble explaining yourself, and yelling at us to buy Bioamerica. You wouldn't let anyone else talk. Remember - you staggered home."

"Jesus Christ! How can this happen?" The secretary asks, "What's the current price of Bioamerica?"

The President locates the stock quotes from Morningstar .com on the computer to see its $20 a share. The secretary demands the president make a presidential decision and sell Bioamerica today before it drops down below what F.I.C paid for it.

Trevor Goodman (having a little fun with his secretary) tells Gary Glenn he has officially resigned earlier this morning. If the secretary wants to call everyone up and explain the situation, including the news of the president's resignation, it would be appreciated. Plus, I expect a plaque for all the time and efforts that I put into the investment club.

"You call Susan and sell Bioamerica now, and I'll call everyone to tell them what happened, and I wish you would resign you son of a bitch," screams the secretary in the phone.

BENNY BENSON

Benny Benson had to be tough in his childhood, for everyone picked on the smallest kid to fight. He probably caused most of his problems by speaking his mine, nothing wrong with that, unless no one was there to back you up. A successful business man, he started with a small fitness club and made good. His Joe Pesci's style of conversation actually brought customers in to hear what outrageous remarks he would make towards them or on world issues - people couldn't get enough of his act. Benny was so successful, he thought about a bigger place, offering tennis, swimming and fitness. He decides to sell the fitness club at a huge profit and build the only total fitness center in town.

His sister-in law worked as a secretary for FAN radio, a sports station out of New York. Knowing the president was a big New York Giants fan, he invites Trevor Goodwin to a playoff game in December. The weather was warm, almost sixty degrees, unbelievable according to Benny who almost froze to death at previous playoff games. Lifting the cover off of his small pickup truck, out came folding chairs, a charcoal grill, a cooler, a football and a wheel chair.

The president asks, "Why the wheel chair?"

"You'll see," answers Benny Benson.

After eating, drinking, and throwing the football around in the parking lot, it was time to go inside to see the game.

Benny sets up the wheel chair by unfolding it, and instructs the president that he just has to push him up several spiral flights of stairs to get to the handicap seats on level four of the stadium. The stadium allows one handicap person and an aide to seat in special areas of the stadium.

"You're not serious?" asks Trevor Goodman.

"Don't worry about a thing. I work with a disabled guy who is going to meet us at gate twenty. He's a season ticket holder and owes me a favor – plus he claims there're plenty of seats available for disabled people that are never used."

"What about the ten people next to us who saw me throwing you football passes just minutes ago?"

"Listen, the seats are unbelievable, right at the fifty yard line. Our free tickets are way up near the roof. Look around, we're the only ones left in the parking lot."

"So how are we going to be allowed into the handicap area with our roof tickets?"

Benny's cell phone rings, and his co-worker says its time to get moving.

"We're going to gate twenty, our gate, but the attendants are going to inform us that seats are available for wheel chair occupants, and we just follow their suggestion as if we didn't know those seats were available."

"I'm not doing this," says Trevor Goodman.

"If you want to see the game, you're doing it," answers Benny Benson. "My disabled buddy is going to meet us at the gate, and he'll help us with getting in."

"I can't believe I'm doing this. Just promise me you won't jump out of your wheel chair when the Giants score or start the wave in the handicap section."

"I'm glad you said that. Make sure I stay in my wheel-chair through out the game."

Benny was almost killed by Mario Bossi (at Steve Culcarta's cottage) when he reacted to Mario's gambling addiction. Playing the same four digit lotto numbers every day didn't make any sense –especially 0000. "It must be the Agent Orange that blew into your nose and lungs from the helicopter blades in Vietnam that causes you to snap and lose it mentally," says Benny Benson to Mario's face. He also adds, "The Vietnam War was stupid and worthless." It took all of the members to keep Mario from killing Benny – who never mentioned the Vietnam War again.

He got on everybody's nerves with his attitude and harsh comments, but lucky for him, he selected a stock named Red Alert that will bring in thousand of dollars for F.I.C.

MARIO BOSSI

Mario Bossi's number was called to serve in Vietnam. A decorated helicopter pilot, he would return to serve a second time. Mario was a big time gambler, and constantly filled his wallet on a weekly basis with lotto tickets. He played the horses, went to casinos, bet on sport teams, and unlike many gamblers he won more than he lost. Playing the stock market was gambling, so he was interested. A huge man, he had no problem with the physical demands placed on a mason. A hard worker, he eventually took over a friends business by purchasing the company outright. You had to be stupid to mess around with Mario - that's why the bookies always paid Mario his money.

While visiting Mario at a construction site to pick up used bricks, Jim O'Sullivan and Trevor Goodman experienced a frightful situation. As Jim backed up his pick up truck following Trevor's directions, they heard a truck backfire. Why was everyone laying on the ground? Another truck or the same truck backfired again. That's when Mario runs over to tell both men to hide inside the nearest bucket loader, someone is shooting at the construction site. Mario explains he's been winning a lot of bets lately, and hasn't been paid, so he put a lot of pressure on the "man" who's returning the favor. He's going to call Luigi to fix the problem. Jim and Trevor left immediately without any bricks.

Mario Bossi arranged a bus trip between F.I.C members and a local union of masons for a trip to an UConn vs. Providence men's basketball game in Providence, R.I. The bus holds 40 passengers, 2 metal trash cans filled with cold beer, card board boxes filled with Subway grinders, boxes of cigars, and extra cases of beer stored up in the luggage racks, with Motown music blasting from the bus speakers.

The bus driver was black, talked with a deep southern accent, which no one could understand, and tipped the scales at 300lbs. He enjoyed the music so much that whenever a Temptations song came on, the bus speed would increase to 95 mph.

The 2hr trip caused problems with passenger bladders and restroom usage. Some passengers had to urinate out the back windows because some one was passed out in the only restroom on board.

About a half hour from our destination, the bus driver decides to hit the brakes hard to avoid a collision with a disabled vehicle. This emergency action saves the passengers lives,but unfortunately for the bus driver, the cases of beer stored up in the luggage rack flew forward - hitting the driver in the back of the head, knocking him unconscious for a few seconds. Many passengers are also injured due to the driver's actions.

Since the game wasn't going to start for another 45 minutes, F.I.C members followed some of the masons a couple of blocks to a topless bar. After the first and second dancers finished their performances a beautiful dancer (Venus) started the third dance of the evening at about the same time the basketball game started in the Donkin Donut center. Since there were no T.V.'s in the bar, no one realized the game had started.

Venus was a very talented, gorgeous dancer, and some of the F.I.C members wanted to stay and see her perform a second time, since it was announced that the next performance included a partner and a fire pole. When she finally came back on stage, the place seemed empty, and the members of F.I.C thought the men who left had missed the best act of the evening.

After her academy award performance, she comes off the stage to greet the F.I.C members who have been very generous with tips during her performance and sits her half naked body next to Mike Chitkowski - asking him if he would like a lap dance? While she is dancing on his lap he loses it, and starts to kiss and grab her, which is not allowed. This bouncer quickly comes over and grabs Mike by the throat to inform him about the rules of engagement. This guy was huge, but for some unknown reason, one of the masons whose forearms were bigger than most peoples thighs, decided to deck the bouncer for disrupting the performance, which in turn caused another bouncer to back up the first, causing other masons with larger forearms to back up the first mason, causing a barroom brawl.

The next thing the members of F.I.C knew everyone was outside while trying to regroup before the cops came. Many patrons made it outside except Mike Chitkowski, Mario Bossi and some masons who were cuffed by police inside the bar. The funniest sight was watching the police escort Mike and Venus, both cuffed together, and enjoying each other's company to the police station.

It was time to go to the game, but first someone had to bail out Mike and Mario. Of course no one wanted to bail out people from jail - since the game was in the third period – the members of F.I.C felt it was the President's position to bail out any members in trouble. Plus they weren't going to miss the whole game because of them. Trevor Goodman demanded the members of F.I.C accompany him to bail out Mike and Mario or he'll resign. They tell him to resign, their not missing the basketball game. "You're the President, you bail them out."

By the time Mike Chitkowski and Mario Bossi were freed from jail, Mike asked Venus to marry him, the game was over and the bus, carrying the members of F.I.C, had left Providence. Now the three members of F.I.C had to find a ride home. They went back to the spot were the buses parked. Four buses were still waiting for passengers to arrive, so they approached each bus, hoping one was going back to Connecticut. The last bus driver said the bus was going to East Hartford, Ct. and if they can't find the six remaining passengers, then room will be available for a charge of $40 a piece. He said the bus leaves in 10 min. if no one else shows.

While waiting outside the bus, the President and his F.I.C buddies look up at the windows to see what the passengers looked like. They were all senior citizens. The trip home is going to be a lot quieter than the one that brought them here. No beer or grinders on board this bus.

The bus driver said to come aboard, there's always seniors who get on the wrong bus or forget were a bus is parked. Its time to head back to Ct. All the passengers seemed to be sleeping or lacked a pulse as Mario Bossi observed while the F.I.C members looked for seats.

The President calls the other members of F.I.C on their cell phones to tell them they boarded another bus and need a ride from East Hartford to West Hartford to get back to their cars. Only one member answers the phone and Jim O'Sullivan tells the President he can't talk to him right now because he's in a poker game that needs his focus, call back in a few minutes. The President gets through to Benny Benson and tells him the situation, asking him if he knew what highway they were on. Maybe the buses can stop at an exit and they can get back on the right bus.

Benny Benson says, "Their not on a highway – were on some side road – where are you?"

"We're on a bus filled with senior citizens -no beer or food- heading towards East Hartford by rt.2 south."

Benny Benson starts to yell to people in the back round what he just heard from Trevor Goodman and adds while laughing, "I need to get off the phone to take a leak, that is the funniest story I've ever heard, call me back in a few minutes."

Mario Bossi and Mike Chitkowski want to know from the President if he's talked to F.I.C members on the other bus to make connections? Trevor Goodman responds, "I'm trying to get through to the idiots that keep hanging up on me. See if anybody has anything to drink, I could use a beer right now." The President tries the cell phone of Benny Benson again and tells him to give the phone to the driver of the bus.

"What for?" asks Benny Benson –who could hardly be heard because of all the background noise.

"So I can have our driver talk to your driver to see if we can get back on the right bus," answers the President.

The bus drivers determined that it would be impossible to meet since each bus was traveling on two different roadways.

Mike Chitkowski tells the President that one of the senior passengers said to drink his specialty drink, it always makes him feel good. At this point, the President needed a drink - so he takes what appears to be a shot glass and drinks it down. "What did I just drink?" asks Trevor Goodman. The answer comes from Mike, "prune juice and vodka - want some more?"

The Presidents cell phone rings and Benny Benson is on the other line. He just called a mailman friend of his in East Hartford who'll pick them up at their drop off location. (He will be driving a mail truck) Put the bus driver on the phone to speak to his East Hartford connection then get back on the phone, you need to be sitting down when I tell you what is going on inside this bus.

After the driver and the pick up person finish talking, the President gets back on the phone to ask Benny what's happening. He tells the President that one of the dancers from the strip joint is on board and is good friends with Venus.

"We told her Mike is very rich, and maybe Venus could hook up with Mike. She tells us Venus is very male. Mike kissed and groped a guy! Venus is a guy - can you believe it? Don't tell Mike until we get back home, we want to see his face when he finds out."

Trevor Goodman is in shock, but proceeds to tell Mario Bossi and Mike Chitkowski, a dancer from the strip club is on board their bus, she's friends with Venus, and she wants to get together with Mike when they get home. Mike tells the President he is going to be the best man at the wedding. Trevor wants to tell Mike the truth, but instead responds, "I can't wait to see how dishearten the other members will be when they hear I'm the best Man at the wedding - stressing the word man." All three of them ask the old geezer for another prune juice and vodka to celebrate.

Mario selects Industrial Gaming as a stock for consideration at next months meeting.

STEVE CULCARTA

He would give you the shirt off his back, and didn't charge you full price if you were his friends, unfortunately that's not the way to run a business. The youngest member at thirty years old, Steve Culcarta left high school in his junior year to work with his oldest brother painting cars. He was so successful in auto body repair, especially aluminum welding, Ford offers him a position in Detroit, working on the new Ford Cobra model. A heavy smoker and under pressure to work thirty extra hours a week with the Ford Cobra racing team, Steve decides to partner up with a friend to purchase a auto body shop in town, start a family, and work normal hours. The cars were lined up at his shop and satisfied customers were scheduling repairs from morning to night. Steve and his partner were making lots of money. He purchased a beautiful house, a lake cottage, and a new Ford Cobra.

Yearly, Steve would host a Super bowl party and invite the members of F.I.C to stay at his lake front cottage for a three day weekend of drinking and partying.

It was Jim O'Sulivan who brought up the idea of having a F.I.C get together at Steve Culcarta's cottage in Tolland, Connecticut. No one knew of his ownership of a cottage on Tolland lake, yet the news was some how attained by Jim and breaking his vow of silence, everyone else now wanted to see the place.

Steve Culcarta tried to politely explain all the reasons why the members of F.I.C would never be invited to the lake, but one stood out among the others – they drink too much. Yet, he knew he had a workforce of seven people who if sober could help him with a new storm wall he wanted to build down near the edge of his property. So, the deal was, everyone leaves work on Friday to construct wall, return on Sunday night, no drinking. In return for this favor, the members can party at his cottage - he'll supply the food and entertainment. The wall came out better then anyone could imagine. The members were shown a wave runner, water tube, and speedboat that were on the entertainment list to use the next time they came.

As the members started to look at the calendar to arrange the weekend get away, Steve Culcarta put a wrench into the planning. He never said weekend – there's too many people at the lake on weekends – the party has to be during the week when his neighbors aren't there. The best time would be arriving Thursday night and leaving Sat morning.

The first response came out of the mouth of Gary Glenn, "I can't take time off during the week, I'm a traveling sales man, and my back still hurts from building your freaking wall."

"It's going to be hard for everyone to take time off, but I understand your concerns about having us at your cottage and I do appreciate the invitation – so if it's not on a weekend, then count me out," expresses Trevor Goodman.

"Don't give us that understanding crap," announces Jim O'Sullivan. He implied it was going to be a weekend deal – he has to fulfill his promise or will throw his ass out of F.I.C."

Appearing angry, Trevor Goodman stands up and walks out of the meeting as if he was never coming back. He walks around the block - turns around and enters the building from the side entrance. As he re-enters the meeting room to announce his resignation, he notices Mike Chitkowski is missing.

Within minutes, a nervous, out of breath Mike Chitkowski comes in telling the President to, "Sit down – have a beer – everything's o.k. – we're all going to the cottage three weeks from today – on a weekend. I tried to find you."

The President tells the group that if he ever walks out again, then that's it, you'll never have me as president again. Winking at Steve Culcarta, everyone but Mike Chitkowski realized it was all a set up.

The van was filled with cases of beer, fishing equipment, food, and a video camera. Driving the van was Benny Benson, who asks the passengers not to drink until the group arrived at the lake. He didn't want everyone getting a head start on the alcohol consumption.

He barely finished his request when the first beer can was snapped opened, approximately one half hour into the drive, the beer count had started. By the time the hour and a half trip ended, a full case of beer was gone and several members were intoxicated.

As the van pulls into the driveway, the members jump out of the van and begin to urinate in some small bushes next to the cottage. This was video taped by Benny Benson who also noticed that the members were missing the bushes and urinating on their sneakers while they discussed the lay out of the property – not focusing on the task at hand.

Talking loudly, they were told to keep their voices down by Steve Culcarta, who comes out the front door to greet his fellow members carrying a red cup with a S & D logo on the side, filled with vodka and coke –cola. Noticing them urinating on his bushes he reminds the members that restrooms are available in the cottage in case the urge comes again.

Everyone now unpacks the van; proceeds down to the patio in the back of the cottage to continue to drink, eat snacks, light up a few cigars, and listen to our tour guide

(Steve Culcarta) explain the agenda for the next two days. Sitting on the patio table was a huge trophy that would be awarded to the winner of F.I.C's first fishing tournament. Our tour guide points to a 20 ft. speedboat tied to the dock, which is now going to take us around the lake.

Since most of the members were intoxicated from the time they arrived until they left the lake, it was fortunate that the video camera was always found in time to capture on film, the most hilarious lake moments. For example, Trevor Goodman, drunk, listening to music on the radio doing his weight lifting poses as if he were in competition – using tree stumps, lawn chairs, and picnic tables.

Tube rides, where a large tire tube was attached to the speedboat as each member of F.I.C took turns trying to hold on for their lives, while the boat reached record speeds. Using hand signals to tell the boat operator to slow down, speed up, stop, signals that were ignored by intoxicated members in the boat, including the driver who was DWI at the time.

Benny Benson just missed hitting the dock when someone in the boat mis-took the signal as a turn signal when Benny was trying to signal he had lost his bathing suit. Along with the bathing trunks, an expensive watch, money, wedding ring, and several hats were lost tubing across the lake. All captured on film.

A lot of video time, unfortunately, was taken of members urinating at different times of the day, all over the property. One is pissing on the lamppost, another on the neighbors ceramic duck family, on the dock, in the ditch next to the cottage, standing in the boat, on the tool shed, in the water-forming a circle while talking to each other about how cool it was to be able to urinate in their pants and the final camera shot – a master piece – video camera left on the new storm wall pointing at the whole group urinating together to put out the camp fire while looking up at the sky trying to see shooting stars.

The speedboat was now boarded for the sunset lake tour. The boat headed east following the longest part of the lakeshore, then headed north into some coves and inlets that would hold the trophy fish caught the next day by Mike Chitkowski and Trevor Goodman. As the boat headed west towards the public beach area – our tour guide (Steve Culcarta) suddenly puts the boat into full throttle as we passed what appeared to be a building with a neon beer sign in the window. The boat seemed to be traveling at the speed of light away from the building and beach, but if you looked quickly by turning your head against the wind, you could see signs next to the building indicating happy hour, pool tables, keno, and karaoke.

As the lake tour ended and the boat was tied to the dock – one of the members – guess who – quickly questions the tour guide by asking if that was a bar we passed going full throttle near the public beach.

"No," answered Steve Culcarta. "That place has been closed for years."

" Are you sure?" questions Benny Benson, "Because I saw a beer truck parked next to the building's front door."

"That's a grocery store," responds Steve Culcarta.

"I think you're lying," states Benny Benson. "Anyone else see the bar and its signs?"

Trevor Goodman didn't answer, but he also saw the bar and its signs.

"You tried to avoid us seeing the place – that's why you gunned the boat in the opposite direction "– argued Benny Benson.

"Why would I do that?" questions Steve Culcarta.

"Your afraid of us going over to the bar and causing trouble with the locals – aren't you?"

"We're not going near that bar – its trouble – last month the resident state trooper was called in to stop a fight – we're not going near that bar!" demands Steve Culcarta.

"Says who – your not our mother," blurted Benny Benson.

"No one is going near that bar, end of discussion," screams Steve Culcarta, while drinking his vodka and coke down in one gulp as he looks at the president for help.

Trevor Goodman hates being president, but being a leader he asks for a vote – "Raise your hands if you want to" – all the hands goes up before he even finishes his request.

"Do any broads hang out at the bar?" questions Mike Chitkowski.

Steve Culcarta didn't respond – only shook his head in disgust.

As darkness fell, the members of F.I.C board the boat to travel about ten minutes over to the bar on the other side of the lake.

There was hardly anyone in the bar when F.I.C arrived – just a few locals sitting at the bar eating their boiled eggs while drinking beer from the tap. Things were going fine as far as the tour guide was concerned - until some women entered the bar about the same time Mike Chitkowski was feeling good and high. He was teamed up with the President at the pool table because no one else wanted him as a partner when one of the women looked at the President and decided to tell him he looked a lot like Tom Cruise. He still doesn't know why he answered her by telling her he was Tom Cruise – but he did.

Suddenly Steve Culcarta announces the boat was leaving in five minutes and warned everyone to not miss boarding. "We are getting up early tomorrow because of the fishing tournament."

The women were rated from 7 to 10 on the beauty scale and all three were in the 7 range. Mike Chikowski asks the bartender if they were local or visitors. The bartender said they were locals and the one talking to your friend is married. "How about the other ones?" asked Mike Chitkowski. The bartender said, "he's not sure."

Mike informs Trevor Goodman what he learned from the bartender just as the tour guide announced it was time to leave.

"Let's stay," asks Mike.

"No," answers Trevor.

The other members of F.I.C start to get involved by telling Mike they'll come back to pick them up if he wanted to stay and try his luck with the girls – which was a lie.

Steve Culcarta tells the Treasurer no one is coming back. "Let's go."

The boat was about half way across the lake when Steve Culcarta notices lights were on his neighbor's cottage. This needed to be checked out because his neighbor never visits the lake during the first two weeks of September – plus local teenagers have been breaking into cottages to party when no ones around.

As the boat slips into the dock Steve Culcarta notices his neighbor's car is parked to the side of the cottage, usually it's parked in the front driveway. Steve informs the group to quiet down and carefully exit the boat while he goes next door to check things out.

The President informs Steve that it's almost 1am in the morning, maybe you should wait until tomorrow. Steve disagrees, something isn't right, he asks the President to go with him to check on his neighbor.

It doesn't take long for Steve and Trevor to reach the neighbor's cottage. Steve looks inside to see if the neighbor is there. No one seems to be inside and everything inside seems to be normal.

Trevor Goodman asks, "How old is the guy?"

"About our age," answers Steve. "I don't see any movement, so I guess he's asleep. I'll check on him tomorrow like you suggested," whispered the concerned neighbor.

Trevor Goodman was the first person awake and he walks down to the lakefront to encounter a magnificent sunrise. Standing alone, focusing on the calm lake water, a slight breeze hits his sleepy face. He's looking for signs of fish rising for flies on the water's surface. Imagine witnessing this natural phenomenon everyday, peaceful-almost spiritual, it feels good to be alive.

In the distance, floating on the water, a family of ducks feed together as they move from the center of the lake towards him. The sounds of waves, in a steady cadence, gently hitting the shoreline, mixed in with birds singing their morning songs filled the air. The sounds of frogs croaking nearby, bounces off his eardrums – close sounds of frogs – very close frogs. The frogs were making different sounds – maybe some were female and the other males.

Someone behind him burps and farts out loud. It's Mike Chitkowski who now farts and burps again while saying good morning to the President.

"You went to bed earlier then everyone else – you missed the porno films last night and I'm your partner for today's fishing tournament." In one hand he's holding a fishing pole and in the other a can of beer and a donut. The President now wonders if he actually heard the sound of frogs or something else.

The fishing tournament was on – everyone was paired up with a partner except Steve Culcarta who didn't like to fish. Trevor and Mike, Benny and Mario, Gary and Jim, all in rented boats, fishing for the big trophy. Steve Culcarta would drive his wave runner back and forth from one boat to the other, supplying the fisherman with beer and updates as to who was leading in the tournament.

Trevor and the Mike just pulled into a cove when a huge fish hits a fly on the surface of the water.

The excited Treasurer asks, "Did you see what I just saw?"

"Yes I did," answered the President. "Cut the engine and let's drift into the area as quietly as we can."

Trevor and Mike were gliding the boat slowly and quietly as each cast fell closer to the fish.

"Thank God you're a fly fisherman – if you hook this one, the trophy is ours," says a confident treasurer.

The President casts are perfect, and the fish starts to take interest in the Adam's fly he's using. Just when the fish turns to make a run at the fly a huge splash is heard behind the boat.

In the near distance, someone is diving off a boat into the water. On closer inspection, it's a female in a bikini, and the other person driving the boat is also a female wearing a bikini. The female driver is now throwing an anchor over board and diving into the water.

"Their goes our chances of winning the tournament," states a disgruntled President. No sooner did the words come out of the President's mouth than the boat driven by Mike Chitkowski was headed towards the two females. Trevor Goodman tried to reason with him about winning a fishing tournament, but that was not on the mind of the treasurer. "Let me do the talking," demanded Mike Chitkowski.

As the boat approaches the female swimmers, the treasurer looks at the president and says, "Do you recognize the broads?"

Trevor answers, "Yes I do."

"That's the married broad and her friend from last night. I wonder if they recognize us?" questions Mike.

"Hello," shouts Mike, "Nice to see you again, enjoying your morning swim?"

"Good morning – yes we are. Catch any fish," asks the married female, directing the question to the president.

"It's a little noisy around here to catch a fish," explains an angry angler.

"Sorry about that." The two females now climb back into the boat exposing their athletic bodies to the fisherman. "We'll move to another location so you can catch the big one."

"Talking about a big one whispers Mike to the president. I'm getting excited looking at their bodies. Check out the single broads body, she's a ten not a seven."

"I agree," answers Trevor.

"The married one's body is pretty nice too. "I agree," answers the president again.

"We're sorry about the noise, if we can get this engine started, will be on our way – it's been hard to start all morning." The single female gives the rope a pull and no response from the engine. She tries again and black smoke comes pouring out of the engine.

Mike Chitkowski, seeing a golden opportunity, offers to come aboard to start the engine which just needs the use of the choke. The two females tell the treasurer if he can start the engine, they would appreciate it. He can't get the engine started, because they have no oil in the engine - he's lying. He quickly offers to tow them back to the cottage to get the free oil they need. They agree to the offer. The president and the treasurer are now towing the two bikini clad females back to the cottage.

As the two boats start their journey back to the cottage, two helicopters begin to circle the lake at low altitudes. Both helicopters (T.V. and State Police) seem to be hovering over Steve's cottage says Trevor to Mike. Mike also notices Steve Culcarta on his wave runner moving fast towards the cottage from the opposite side of the lake. "What the hell is going on?" asks Mike.

The closer the two boats got to the cottage, the more police action they witnessed. Police where everywhere surrounding the neighbor's cottage. Some were positioned on the property and some were on the dock of the cottage visibly holding weapons in their hands.

"Holy shit!" "Do you see what I'm seeing?" asks Trevor Goodman. "Look the other guys are coming in with their boats – I wonder if their catch is as big as ours?"

Steve Culcarta is now speeding towards the boats in his wave runner. He pulls along side the boats and starts to explain what's going on.

"His neighbor told him this morning he was divorcing his wife officially this week and she threaten to take the cottage from him in the divorce settlement. He wasn't going to let her and her boyfriend take the cottage from him, since he built the place with his own blood, sweat, and hands."

"So he decides to pour gasoline on the cottage threatening to burn the place down. I saw him and tried to reason with him to stop pouring gasoline on his cottage when he started to scream and talk nonsense while holding matches in his hand. So I called the cops and told them he was going nuts – somebody better get over here fast. The next thing I know we're live on CNN, all the local stations, and there are helicopters and swat teams on my property, because my neighbors cheating wife told the police her husband has a pistol in the cottage."

"We're all on T.V. according to a neighbor who called on my cell phone right after my wife called me to confirm she also saw all of us on T.V. She wanted to know who the two women being towed across the lake by Mike and Trevor were. My wife wanted to know if there were additional woman around that she should know about."

The first thing Trevor wanted to do was kill Mike, but the police were everywhere, including above their heads. He will murder the treasurer later.

The other fisherman weren't happy about the pictures broadcasting on T.V. and thanks to Mike – they're going to have to explain the situation to their wife's too. Yet, the members of F.I.C were staring at the female bodies sitting in the boat wondering how the hell both parties came together.

"Why didn't I resign?" laments the president as he looks up at the TV helicopter.

The members of F.I.C received many copies of the T.V. videos from all of their close friends when they got back to work.

The president and treasurer won the fishing trophy - which had two female figures added to it, each holding on to two large fishing poles.

Steve Culcarta decides to select Gyrotest as his stock of choice for next months meeting.

JIM O'SULLIVAN

Jim O'Sullivan was a violent child, always in trouble, until he started playing football. His aggressive behavior and fierce competitive nature allowed him to succeed as a football player and coach. At five foot five, strong upper body, he wouldn't back down from any confrontation.

A couple of college punks cut in line ahead of Jim at the movie theater while purchasing tickets. Trevor Goodman noticed the incident while standing in the lobby of the theater with his wife and Jim's wife. By the time Trevor got to Jim and the college punks, Jim was asking them if they liked hospital food. They both moved to the back of the line.

Jim O'Sullivan was recognized by the Connecticut High School Football Association as coach of the year three times. Jim was recruited by Syracuse University in his junior year of high school. Unfortunately, as a senior, he tore his right knee apart playing in his last high school game. The injury was so severe, he needed knee replacement.

Quick witted, he would crack up everyone with his words of wisdom. For an example, when he played golf with Trevor Goodman and Gary Glenn, whoever was losing to Jim got the following suggestion: "Take a couple of weeks off from golf and then quit."

Jim O'Sullivan wasn't the healthiest member of F.I.C., and on several occasions he has been hospitalized with sudden illnesses. The members of F.I.C witnessed him having a kidney stone attack during a meeting. This medical emergency scared the hell out of the president.

Trevor Goodman (a part time Am. Red Cross instructor) immediately sprung into action – telling Gary Glenn to stop eating and call 911 – then his wife.

"Why do you want me to call your wife?" questions Gary who is ten times over the legal limit of intoxication.

"Not my wife, his wife!" Screams the president, who decides to call 911 and Jim O'Sullivan's wife himself. Trevor Goodman then proceeds to ask the ill member questions concerning his emergency while he's still conscious. He's in severe pain and barely able to speak, but he tells the president it's a kidney stone attack.

Another intoxicated member, Benny Benson, asks Jim O'Sullivan (who he thinks is having a heart attack) if he can have his canoe if he dies. This sets off a domino effect around the conference table with other intoxicated members asking for his new golf clubs, snow blower, fishing equipment, and even his wallet.

This angers the president and he loudly informs everyone to sober up, because we have a real emergency on our hands. If they don't listen to his directions he's going to resign as soon as this emergency is over.

"We're not giving pepperoni breath mouth-to-mouth" states an intoxicated Mario Bossi, followed by "I hear sirens, I wonder what's on fire?"

Mike Chitkowski informs Jim who is now on a stretcher that it's his turn to bring snacks and beer to next months meeting – "unless you can't make it."

Steve Culcarta whispers into Jim's ear as he leaves the room with the paramedics, "if you die – it's going to be for a long time."

Thank God it was winter – the large coats came in handy for hiding beer. The shocked patient was one day away from being released. The last thing he needed or wanted was the members of F.I.C visiting him in the hospital.

The first F.I.C member to enter room 416 was Benny Benson – who quickly announces the guests can only stay a couple of hours, while he throws his coat over the T.V. The second person to enter the room was Mario Bossi who is dumping a bucket of ice into the sink to keep the ice beer cold. Next person in was Mike Chitkowski who accidentally knocks the patient's medical charts off the wall while holding onto a vase of red roses. Following behind Mike is Gary Glenn who wants to know if the patient has eaten dinner yet, he's starving. Steve Culcarta is now opening a can of ice beer and about to light a cigarette when the patient screams at him to stop, there's oxygen in the room.

The President is just about to talk, when an angry intern comes in screaming at Mike Chitkowski to return the vase and flowers to room 415 or he'll call security. Mike apologizes and informs the intern – we thought the patient in room 415 was dead. The guests quickly stand in front of the sink, blocking the intern's view of the beer.

Mario Bossi, who is helping put the medical charts back on the wall, notices the charts didn't have Cealis listed – so he adds See-Alice to each chart – approximately 100 grams daily.

Everyone has an ice beer in his hands and the President is speaking on behalf of all the members of F.I.C by wishing Jim O'Sullivan a speedy recovery when Nurse Cashman bursts in.

She is six feet tall, weighing over 200lbs, looks a lot like Hulk Hogan in a nurse's uniform, and screams at the patient who is drinking beer to "Put the beer down. What is wrong with you people? It's against hospital rules to have beer in a hospital. Everyone has to leave now and don't come back – visiting hours are over."

Benny Benson starts to collect the beer from the sink when Hulk Hogan grabs him by the collar and says – "the beer stays right where it is or she'll call security."

Jim O'Sullivan thanks the members for coming in and tells them he's going home tomorrow. Nurse Cashman tells the patient, "You're not being released tomorrow. Your blood pressure is still too high." She grabs the beer and medical charts and walks back to the nurse's station in disgust.

When healthy, Jim O'Sullivan amazed the others with his math skills. He could figure out a stock's balance sheet, each member net worth, percent profit for each stock on a yearly, monthly, and weekly basis, within minutes. Within seconds, he could also tally up the gambling debts owed him by fellow members who were stupid enough not to pay him.

Since this member's math skills were above the comprehension of others, he was assigned the task of devising a system F.I.C could use to automatically buy and sell stocks.

Convincing the members to automatically buy and sell stocks at a certain price didn't get the immediate approval of all members, but he was able to find a common denominator between members who couldn't decide when to purchase or sell a stock.

His system included "cut off price" (auto sell) when a stock rose 10% to 15% above the purchase price – (auto buy) when stock price dropped 25% below its 52 wk high. Since F.I.C wasn't dealing with huge amounts of cash or short-term transactions – this system seemed to work.

Jim O'Sullivan bought a boat and invited Trevor Goodman to fish the shoreline of Connecticut for blues and strippers. This was the first time he was using the boat since taking the required coast guard boating course.

As they left the marina, the Captain (Jim O'Sullivan's new name) started to bark out orders to Trevor Goodman, starting with setting up the radio antenna on the side of the boat. Trevor obliges as the Captain drives his 20' boat towards the channel out to the open sea.

Within 30 sec. of backing out of his boat slip, while Trevor is trying to figure out how to prop open the antenna, the Captain yells to the president to keep his head down. The President follows his orders and ducks his head down for a few seconds and then lifts his head to see a pulpit from a parked sailboat just miss crushing his head. He asks the Captain why he steered the boat so close to the other boats. The answer was, the current was stronger than he thought it would be in a marina. Just as he finishes speaking an alarm goes on and off under the boats control center. The Captain looks at all the gages and casually says everything is normal, must be a loose connection and proceeds to point the boat towards the channel. The two boaters drink their first ice beers, celebrating a day of fishing versus working.

According to his fishing map, the best fishing spot is through the channel heading to the west around the first buoy marker. As the boat enters the end of the channel, a large boat is traveling fast directly at the boat. Both the president and the Captain notice the huge boat at the same time. The Captain now informs the scared president that the huge boat must yield the right of way, since the boating course he just finished says all boats must enter the channel on the right side of the red buoys.

Trevor Goodman now points out to the Captain that all the other small boats are getting out of the way of the huge boat and maybe we should do the same thing. Even though the huge boat might be on the wrong side of the buoy, it could easily kill us if we collide. At the last minute, the Captain decides to yield the way to the huge boat, who is so close to his boat that voices of the men on board the huge boat could be heard screaming, "Get on the left side of the red buoys asshole." The boat now safely rounds the channel just as the alarm goes on and off again under the control center.

"I wonder why the alarm keeps going off?" asks the Captain. He tells Trevor to drive the boat while he investigates the problem. He's looking for the operator's manual when the President tells him to look at the action on the surface of the water. There's baitfish all around the boat and schools of strippers are in a feeding frenzy. Birds are diving out of the sky feeding on baitfish, as the two boaters grab their fishing poles. The hell with the alarm, cut the engine, it's time to fish.

Within 15 minutes, the President hooks on to two 32" strippers on lightweight fly tackle, just like you see on the sports channel. The action was unbelievable and attracted other boats to the area. The President catches several more fish – not realizing the boat has drifted further out to sea. The Captain who hasn't caught a fish, because he's using a spinning reel is ticked off, but restarts the engine to get the boat back into position where the fish were biting.

The engine starts, but the alarm goes on, and stays on. The boat with the alarm blasting, is heading back to the area of action when the engine dies out. Unfortunately, the Captain didn't warn Trevor Goodman who was about to sit down to read the operators manual, that he was going to put the engine in full throttle – causing the President to fall backwards into the seat. The force of the boat going forward and the weight of the President going backward acted together to rip the seat out of its base, sending the President flying towards the engine. Thank god the engine shut off; otherwise the President could have been ripped apart from the propellers.

After apologizing to the President and securing the seat to the front rails of the boat, the Captain opens to the trouble shooting section of the operator's manual to locate alarms. There're several reasons for alarms to go off, one of which is the lack of engine oil. He checks the level of oil – empty. Since he didn't have any extra oil on board, he sends out a distress call on his radio. The call is picked up by the towboat service at the marina.

The towboat service informs the Captain - they normally don't bring oil out to boats, just tow them in. "Does he carry insurance?"

"Yes," responds the captain.

"Then that should cover the cost of getting oil out to you. We'll be there in about an hour – set your anchor."

The Captain and Trevor Goodman crack open their second ice beer while waiting for the towboat. In the mean time, bait fish are starting to reappear near the boat. Again, they reach for their poles to start fishing when the Captain notices his pole is missing. His pole costs several hundred dollars and he can't believe it's gone. Where did it go?

He asked the President to place the pole in one of the holders just before the seat incident. He asks the President if he put the rod in the holder.

"Yes," responds Trevor Goodman.

"Then why isn't it in the holder?" asks the Captain.

"I guess it's because the seat must have hit the rod when it broke off the base. Look at the marks from the boat seat; they are in the same spot as the holder. The rod must have gone over board."

"Speaking of going over board, you're lucky I'm not throwing you over," cautioned an angry Captain. Tensions were getting high. A third can of ice beer is consumed by both men.

The towboat radioed they were in visual contact with the boat, and should be next to us in ten minutes, have your insurance card handy. A series of important questions were asked over the radio - needed to fill out insurance form and also to save time. The last question was how much insurance coverage do you have? "Four hundred dollars," answers the Captain.

The towboat ties up to the boat and the operator hands over the needed oil. The towboat operator asks the Captain to sign the form and warns that there's a small craft warning advisory being issued for later this afternoon. I suggest you head back to the marina soon.

The Captain didn't hear the towboat operator's warning because he was looking at the insurance form he just signed over to the operator, indicating the cost of the service is four hundred dollars.

"You're charging four hundred dollars for five quarts of oil?"

"That's right," answers the operator. "Would you rather me tow you in – it's going to cost you three times as much?"

"Thanks, but no thanks. Have a good day," responds the Captain.

The President tries to persuade the Captain to call it a day, "we've been trough a lot today, plus the weather is now a factor."

The Captain asks, "What are you talking about?"

"The towboat operator said to head in to shore now, there's a small craft warning issued for this afternoon."

The boat radio now starts buzzing with the news of albacore tuna being caught within the next buoy from the boat. Many boats are headed directly towards their boat, chasing the tuna towards the Captain and President. With only one pole aboard, a fly pole, which the Captain didn't know how to use, the President decides to ask the Captain if he wanted to try the fly pole. He tries to cast the fly pole, but can't handle the casting technique. The President quickly arranges the fly pole into position, and hooks on to small, but feisty tuna and can't believe the fish came to him. The action lasts for about a half an hour, time enough for the Captain's fourth ice beer.

It is starting to rain, the clouds are darkening, and the waves are getting bigger.

The President can't recall catching so many fish in one day. He tells the Captain, between the boat problems and the fishing, this is going to be a day he'll never forget. He asks the Captain to head back to the marina before they get caught in a storm.

The Captain agrees with the President, sits down in the Captain's seat, and guns the boat again without warning the President who has to hold on to the railing of the control center to keep from falling.

The Captain is upset that he didn't catch any fish, lost an expensive fishing pole, spent four hundred dollars for oil, and is using the speed of his boat to release a lot of tension. The President realizing the problem tells the slightly intoxicated Captain to slow down. Unfortunately, the rain starts to fall heavily along with some lighting and thunder in the distance. The President screams at the Captain to slow down, since waves are coming over the front of the boat, hitting the windshield. The Captain tells the President to relax. According to the previous owner, the boat is built to take a beating.

It was the next wave that cracked the windshield, sending the bolts holding the canopy above the boater's heads into the sea. One of the bolts grazes the President's head, one millimeter away from killing him. With the marina in sight, the President decides not to choke the Captain, and prays the boat can stay in one piece until it reaches the marina. The Captain quickly parks the boat, ties it to the dock, just as all hell breaks lose with lighting and thunder.

The Captain and the President run to the nearest shelter to get out of the storm, which ends up being the towboat station.

PART 2.

THE CURSE

How quickly the months go by, another F.I.C meeting. Susan checks her interoffice mail to retrieve final copies of F.I.C's By- Laws. As she pulls out the pile of papers, a small envelope drops to the floor. Susan picks it up, opens it, and reads the note inside as she walks back to her office. It's from the CFO's assistant; "I'm officially retiring in June, please consider applying for the position – I will help you with this promotion."

A stunned Susan sits in her office chair and rereads the note again and again. Why her? How could she be considered for a promotion when they are several veteran brokers with more seniority and experience? June is only four months away. How can she train for a high level position in only four months?

Susan glances at her office clock, twenty minutes until game time, and Mike Chitkowski hasn't appeared in her doorway. He finally got the message. She rereads the note again and decides to call the CFO's assistant. He assures Susan the position is hers regardless of seniority, because he will train her, plus the CFO wants a women in the position, and not just any woman, he wants her.

"Are you feeling alright? You look a little pale." Mike Chitkowski is standing in Susan's doorway.

She's startled and quickly puts the note back inside the envelope. "I'm fine." Her attention to the note distracted her from securing her office from any visitors.

Mike quickly tells Susan, "I'm not here to ask you out." He's holding a large package. "Please take the time to examine Jim Frond's program, "Strategies for Success." Technology wise it's unbelievable. You can use the information to help your online clients." He gives her the package.

"I'll do that but you hold onto the materials and I'll try to get the firm to purchase the package for me. Can you bring the paper work over to the conference room and set up the room?"

"No problem."

Should she tell Mike that Jim Frond is the CFO's nephew? She decides not to.

Susan is thinking about the promotion as she walks to the conference room. She will double her salary and be released from all responsibilities relating to F.I.C in four months – plus the CFO wants her to fill the position. She can't think of any disadvantages to accepting the offer.

The President is carefully analyzing the data Mike placed in front of him and starts to enjoy his first two ice beers. The members were telling jokes, eating snacks, and drinking while discussing current topics in the news, ignoring the president's actions. Trevor Goodman didn't even notice Susan had entered the room, because his focus was on the list of stocks F.I.C purchased.

Club Golf sold at a $3000 profit, F.I.C reinvested the money at the horse track, losing all $3000.

Bioametric sold at the same price F.I.C paid for it, no gain.

F.I.C bought 100 shares of Sensory Alloy at $2 a share, only to sell the stock at $.50 cents a share. Benny Benson was the only member to install a Sensory Alloy shower head. When his wife went to take a hot shower everything went fine – the shower head automatically shut off and stayed off. She waited for a few minutes and tried to start the shower again- no water. She demanded Benny put the old shower head back on, but he couldn't get the new shower head off – plus he threw the old one out.

The plumber said the reason the Sensory Alloy shower-head didn't come off or produced any additional water was it couldn't be installed on standard fixtures without modifications. He also wanted to know were someone could buy this piece of crap. He's never seen anything like this before. Cost of installing showerhead = $100, price of showerhead = $30.

This incident was reported to all the other members and no one else installed a Sensory Alloy showerhead. A motion was made to send a letter to the company warning them of the problem of installation when giving out samples.

Red Alert sold at a $2,000 dollar profit. F.I.C decided not to reinvest the profits back into purchasing more Red Alert stock as suggested by Susan, but used most of the money for a weekend road trip to a Boston Red Sox game.

It took about a year before the equipment systems used by Gyrotest began to break down. The company had to shut down its testing sites for long periods of time due to faulty equipment. The company was investigated by the Attorney General of Connecticut, due to employees who took bribes from people (to pass test), didn't register their car in Connecticut, and were felons.

Attorney Generals from Massachusetts and New York followed suit when information came out of Connecticut. People reading about the problems with Gyrotest who owned stock in the company started to sell off their holdings. The price of Gyrotest dropped to $.50 cents a share.

Remembering that the last two stocks purchased by F.I.C were disasters, the President warns all the members that F.I.C's purchasing of Industrial Gaming could be its KISS OF DEATH. Plus, not much cash will be left in the account if Industrial Gaming fails. F.I.C votes to purchase Industrial Gaming reminding the President that he told them to keep their heads up high and they will prevail. But he said that thinking they were going to vote for Veggie Burgers and not Industrial Gaming.

After two good months of profits, it took only three months before Industrial Gaming stock started to drop. F.I.C learned that Industrial Gaming was tied into the Mafia, and the president of the company was scheming off of the company's profits. Plus, a few members of the companies board of directors were found shot to death in a Las Vegas parking lot. It was also alleged the machines were rigged to win only on the higher paying machines. The FBI and local law enforcement agencies investigated the company. The decision to sell Industrial Gaming before F.I.C lost all of its money was done at last months meeting.

A pattern of stock failures has now put the investment club into a low cash balance – the lowest amount of money in the account since F.I.C was formed.

The stock that would have made the most money was "Veggie Burgers" – but every time the president offered the stock for a vote he was laughed at. He finishes his first two ice beers and asks for another one as he continues to ponder the information. After finishing his third ice beer Trevor Goodman loudly and angrily announces he's resigning if the members don't select "Veggie Burgers."

This gets the attention of everyone in the room, producing the following responses: 1. "Stop screaming, you look and sound like my wife," 2. "Have another beer asshole" 3.

"Is the meeting starting, we've already wasted a half hour bullshiting." And finally, 4. "I don't see McDonalds selling any Veggie Burgers yet".

"I've mentioned this before when it comes to selecting stocks, and the data proves it, you guys are the "Kiss of Death" There's a pattern here of selecting stocks and I'm not part of it. Look at the information in front of you, there's some strange events surrounding the stocks you selected. I'm the only member to vote NO on stocks that failed and YES on successful buys. I'm begging you guys to break the "KISS OF DEATH CURSE" by purchasing my choice of Veggie Burgers, a stock that has tripled in value."

"I'll bet you twenty dollars that Veggie Burgers fails just like the other stocks," says Mario Bossi.

"I'll take that bet! Anybody else want a piece of the action?" asks Trevor Goodman who is feeling a little buzz from drinking three ice beers.

Interesting thought Susan; no one takes the opportunity of a life time to make twenty dollars.

Trevor Goodman shakes Mario Bossi's hand to seal the bet.

Mike Chitkowski asks Susan, "Do you think we're the "Kiss of Death?"

She's not going to get between the President and the members of F.I.C by taking sides. "Veggie Burgers has tripled in value, it would be interesting to see if it continues to climb. Unfortunately you don't have enough money in the account to buy 100 shares of Veggie Burgers."

"How much money is in the account?" asks Trevor Goodman.

"Only $500," answers Mike Chitkowski

"Including your commission, how much can we buy?"

Susan answers the President, "Twenty shares."

"I make a motion to buy twenty shares of Veggie Burgers to prove a point and win a bet."

Mike Chitkowski seconds the motion.

Trevor Goodman asks, "All in favor?"

All the members vote to purchase twenty shares of Veggie Burgers to prove the President is crazy.

For several weeks, Veggie Burgers stock rose and fell slightly from $20 a share. Then as with the other stocks F.I.C selected it took a nose dive down to $5 a share. The cooking instructions on the packaging were misprinted. Instead of one minute in the microwave, it read seven minutes, over cooking thousands of burgers. A disgruntled employee was found to intentionally program the computers to misprint the instructions. But the stock rebounded after the company corrected the problem, sending the stock back up to $12 a share.

Several members call Trevor Goodman to congratulate him on losing the bet and depleting F.I.C's account balance.

Susan didn't know what to say. She never imagined the timing of F.I.C selections could determine a stocks future, but she's going to take advantage of the situation. She offers the members of F.I.C a choice - continue losing money or disband the investment club. She understands the enjoyment F.I.C members obtain meeting once a month, but comments, "If I were your wives I wouldn't want large amounts of hard earned money going down the drain." She suggests F.I.C disband.

The President, who hated being President, agrees with Susan and announces his resignation. (No one takes his resignation seriously) He adds that his wife actually talked to him last week about F.I.C's failures as an investment club. She said, "You were doomed from the start."

Gary Glenn states, "Susan's right, it's time to quit."

The President thanked Susan on behalf of all the members for her time and efforts.

Susan appreciated the recognition and mentions the firm will send out tax statements for your personal filings. Susan is planning on celebrating F.I.C's decision.

Jim O'Sullivan responds to Trevor Goodman's remarks, "Your right, we appreciate everything you've done Susan and hope you'll be attending our reunions."

Everyone is silently staring at Jim. Did he just say reunions?

Mike Chitkowski breaks the silence. "What a great idea! I make a motion to hold a F.I.C reunion every 3yrs., and I'll promise to help the president organize the events."

Jokingly Jim O'Sullivan sings, "I second that emotion."

Keeping with Smoky Robinson's song title, "I third that emotion" says Gary Glenn.

"I fourth that emotion," continues Mario Bossi. Followed by Steve Culcarta and Benny Benson who fifths and sixths their emotions.

Trevor Goodman reminds everyone, "Sorry guys, I just officially resigned a minute ago."

The seven neighbors leave the firm for the last time as investment club members. Susan is trying to hold back from doing cartwheels.

Exactly a week after F.I.C disbands; Trevor Goodman receives a frantic call from Susan, informing the president that she needs to talk to him ASAP. Trevor asks Susan why the need for a meeting? She answers," You wouldn't believe me if I told you." He meets with her the next day.

As Trevor Goodman enters Susan's office, she asks him if he would like a cup of coffee or soda. He asks for coffee and she leaves the room to prepare it. While she's gone, he looks around the room and down at the paper work piled on top of her desk. Just barely noticeable beneath a stack of letters is a document titled "The KISS OF DEATH CURSE" memo. Trevor Goodman can't believe his eyes. The document was slightly out of alignment with the other letters stacked neatly in one direction, as if this piece of paper was quickly placed in the pile.

Susan reenters the room with his coffee and begins to thank him for responding to her request for a quick meeting and adds –" in a few minutes the Chief Financial Officer of the firm will be coming in to talk to you about a special meeting he wants with F.I.C."

"Why is the Chief Financial Officer interested in talking to the members of F.I.C?"

"You wouldn't believe me if I told you," repeats Susan for the second time.

"Is there a money problem?" asks Trevor.

"No," responds an upset Susan.

Susan continues by talking to herself out loud saying – "I can't believe this is happening"

"Does it have to do with the Kiss of Death Curse F.I.C successfully victimize stocks with?" asks Trevor Goodman while looking down at the memo tucked between the piles of letters.

In a state of shock, Susan stares at Trevor just as the Chief Financial Officer enters the room. He introduces himself to Trevor Goodman and thanks him for coming in. "I asked Susan to contact you about a meeting without informing you of its importance because - frankly we didn't think you would seriously believe us if we told you before hand."

"By collecting data, the firm tracks our four-investment clubs to determine which club is number one in performance. The firm uses this knowledge to make purchases for its own profits. As the Chief Financial Officer, I determine how much money the firm can gain by purchasing the same stocks researched and bought by our investment clubs. However, for the first time in the history of the firm's existence, F.I.C's data shows us its selection of stocks seems to be their Kiss of Death. Yet, the firm can benefit from this phenomenon too. And we have."

Trevor Goodman can't believe what he's hearing. Susan was right – no one could make this up.

The Chief Financial Officer continues; "when F.I.C selected stocks, the firm sold them as quickly as possible; knowing that the Kiss of Death Curse would be in effect, allowing the firm to buy back the shares of stocks at drastically reduced prices. Short selling is especially risky business, unless you know in advance the stock is going to fail, because it entails selling borrowed stocks. (The CFO was a master at returning the borrowed shares to the firm, pocketing the difference between the proceeds of the first sale and the reduced buy back price). The firm used F.I.C's selection of stocks as an indicator of when the stocks would fail – timing is everything."

He didn't quite understand the CFO's explanation of selling short, but the firm thinks F.I.C can predict the future – this is unbelievable ponders Trevor Goodman.

"The firm would like to share the profits with F.I.C, and ask you to explain to F.I.C the firm is willing to purchase the stocks at no cost to the investment club and also purchase snacks and beer for each monthly meeting if F.I.C stays together. Give me your opinion on this offer."

"I'm confused; Susan suggested F.I.C disband, why?" asks Trevor.

"Because she wasn't aware of our actions and desirers until we asked her to call you," explained the Chief Financial Officer. "Give me your opinion."

"If it's legal, the President of F.I.C is o.k. with you presenting the offer to the members of F.I.C., for a vote."

"Good. I'll see you at the meeting and please don't tell your members anything until we meet," requests the Chief Financial Officer. He shakes Trevor Goodman's hand and leaves the room.

Trevor Goodman stands up and tells Susan to make sure everything is legit, and agrees with her that nobody would ever believe what just transpired.

Susan acknowledges everything is legit and hangs her head in disappointment.

Trevor Goodman ignores the request of the CFO and calls for a mandatory meeting at his house.

Trevor informs the membership he met privately with the CFO of the firm a few days ago.

"Why?" interrupts Benny Benson.

"You're not going to believe why, but according to the CFO, F.I.C has been very successful at being unsuccessful. He asked me ...."

"Was Susan at the meeting?" interrupts Mike Chitkowski.

"Yes, but the CFO claims she had no prior knowledge about the offering." answers Trevor Goodman.

"What offering?" interrupts Jim O'Sullivan.

"If you guys let me explain,"continues Trevor Goodman

"Do you believe that she didn't know?" questions Mike.

"Yes. Can I finish explaining what happened again without being interrupted?' asks Trevor Goodman who continues to get interrupted.

"Let me get this straight, you meet with the CFO without us and he wants us to stay together – because we're losers," questions Steve Culcarta.

"Yes, but the he used the words unsuccessful investors."

"Are you on crack?" asks Benny Benson.

"No, but I wondered if the CFO was after hearing him ask me to talk F.I.C out of disbanding. By the way, this meeting never happened or the offer will be rescinded."

"What the hell are you talking about?" asks Gary Glenn.

"The CFO offer, in which he'll explain in detail at our meeting, is too good to refuse. The firm is willing to: purchase stocks we pick, buy beer and snacks, share in their profits, as long as the stock fails – makes our "Kiss of Death hit list". The firm thinks like I do, we hold a CURSE."

"Let's do it. This is unbelievable," screams Mike Chitkowski. Then adds," I hope he doesn't find out about this meeting".

"Make sure they buy enough food and beer," demands Gary Glenn.

"I'll bet everyone $100 bucks that he'll find out about this meeting and resin the offer." Mario Bossi extends his hand for a member to shake – no one does.

"Something isn't right," questions Benny Benson.

"What do you mean?" asks Mike Chitkowski who is concerned the plan won't materialize.

"We don't hold a curse! We're just dumb investors who bought stocks while intoxicated. If something sounds too good to be true, it probably isn't. I think that's the way the saying goes."

Jim O'Sullivan wants to know,"How can anyone make a profit from a failed stock?"

"By short selling" answers Mike Chitkowski.

"How do you know about short selling?' asks Benny Benson.

Mike Chitkowski ignores Benny's question, and feels the need to say, "Let's meet with the CFO and see what happens before we question anything."

Trevor Goodman agrees with Mike, "That sounds logical, I agree with that suggestion."

Everyone else is willing to meet the CFO, but Benny Benson adds, "I can't believe we're doing this, something just doesn't feel right."

Trevor Goodman reminds everyone they have to give their best academy performance when meeting the CFO; they can't tip off the CFO about us meeting.

"What meeting?" answers Mike Chitkowski.

The members of F.I.C are greeted at the conference room door by the CFO, who identifies himself as he shakes each member's hand. They continue to walk towards their seats, having trouble because of the flip charts surrounding the conference table. As the members started to drink the "ice beer" and within seconds, consume about fifty percent of the snacks piled up on the table, they noticed the flip charts used bar and line graphs to indicate the progress of four investment groups labeled #1-4. Except for one chart labeled the Kiss of Death, F.I.C was always at the bottom of every chart.

It took about an hour for the CFO to explain the offer, field questions from the membership, and ask F.I.C to consider what he presented as a serious proposal. Then before leaving, he hands the President a list of names of blue chip stocks the firm wants F.I.C to select from.

Some members question the legality of the offer, and some, especially Mike Chitkowski, think it's a no brainer – "It doesn't cost F.I.C a cent." They all vote to accept the offer.

Now they have to decide which stock they will victimize. The firm's list of stocks contained ten blue chip stocks, including Tyco, Ford, Pfizer, and Enron. Mike Chitkowski convinces the rest of the members to select Pfizer over Enron.

F.I.C selects Pfizer – which the firm quickly short sells 1000 shares at $50 a share. Pfizer announces one month later that it has developed a drug to turn bad cholesterol into good cholesterol. Then Pfizer quickly reverses the findings, stating for the safety of patients tested, the drug failed to work for a large test group off obese adults having high levels of LDL cholesterol, causing unexpected deaths and other complications in the testing phase. However, Pfizer also announces the company will continue to test the drug, confirming they are close to its successful use.

The price of Pfizer drops to $28 a share. Pfizer, after one more month of testing, announces it has successfully developed the drug. The firm buys 1000 shares of Pfizer at $28 a share. The price of the stock goes up to $60 a share.

The members of F.I.C are amazed they have the power to kick in the teeth of a billion dollar company just by selecting it. They started to wonder if they could use their powers in other areas such as horse racing and presidential elections.

The member's of F.I.C select Enron has its next victim. Within days, the firm quickly sells 1000 shares of Enron at $59 a share and specifies a limit order as a day order of $30 a share. The price of Enron plunges to $20 at the end of the trading day.

The selection of Enron destroys the lives of hundreds of people who held Enron stock as part of there retirement accounts. The members of F.I.C didn't own Enron stock, but many of their relatives did.

Enron admitted it disguised bank loans as energy trades in off the books partnerships. Workers were barred from selling their pension fund stocks as Enron collapsed and filed the second largest U.S. bankruptcy in December of 2003.

By F.I.C's selection of Enron, the firm is saved from losing thousands of dollars.

Gary Glenn's and Mario Bossi's parents lost $20,000 and $31,000 within a growth fund designed to be of low risk, because their sons voted to place Enron on the Kiss of Death hit list. The president's brother lost $18,000 in another mutual fund account.

The relatives knew F.I.C existed, but they didn't know about the secret powers they possessed.

This created a dilemma for F.I.C. They need to check with relatives before they selected stocks, but how are they going to do that without divulging their secret agreement with the firm? What if the firm continued to offer F.I.C blue chip stocks owned by relatives?

Mike Chitkowski convinces F.I.C to purchase Ford over Tyco as its next victim. Again, the firm quickly short sells 1000 shares of Ford at $30 a share. Ford and other car companies are showing signs of failure due to the sky rocketing price of gasoline. Within six month's time, Ford announces losing a record 10 million dollars in sales for its first quarter, due to record low sales of F150 pick up trucks. Ford lays off workers and closes plants across the USA. The price of Ford stock drops to $12 a share. The firm buys 1000 shares of Ford at $12 a share. Ford rebounds with the quick delivery of its hybrid Escape Model SUV. Within a year, the price of Ford stock goes up to $40 a share.

Steve Culcarta has two sons who are Ford mechanics that are laid off. Again, F.I.C family members are hurt by the Kiss of Death hit list. A decision needs to be made before another family member suffers the consequences of F.I.C's desires.

F.I.C. selects Tyco next, and it doesn't take long for the members to read the head lines in the paper three months after purchasing it. Two CEO's of Tyco allegedly steal $600 million dollars of company money and use it for plush housing, opulent parties and personal investments. The Kiss of Death Curse continues, the firm and F.I.C continue to make money.

Again, family members are affected by the selection of Tyco by F.I.C.

Since the next time they'll meet is Super Bowl Sunday, it was decided that would be the time to figure out what FIG should do about family vs. the firm when selecting the next Kiss of Death victim.

No one imagined a simple threat directed at Mike Chitkowski by Benny Benson would cause a lengthy discussion about longevity and death among the members of F.I.C.

Benny Benson was upset, because he had to pay Mike Chitkowski $20 for winning the Super Bowl pool. This happened at Steve Culcarta's house. Everyone was intoxicated. Benny Benson didn't mind paying everyone else, but paying Mike Chitkowski was embarrassing.

While accepting his money, Mike calls Benny a loser.

Benny Benson responded by stating the following:"Don't take what I'm about to say personally – drop dead you stupid bastard".

After a few minutes of laughter then silence, Mike Chitkowski continues – "I think you're going to be the first member to drop dead" – looking directly at Jim O'Sullivan who was laughing the loudest.

"What did you just say?" Asks Jim – who starts to move towards the treasurer from the corner of the living room.

Mike continues – "And I think he's going to be the last one of us to die" pointing at the president.

"You're going to drop dead in a few seconds if you don't shut up," exclaims Benny Benson.

Trevor Goodman asks, "Why am I going to die last?"

"Who cares who's going to die first or last, let's drop the subject," butts in the host, Steve Culcarta.

Mike continues, "Because the president's life is more important than ours. He has a purpose in life – he will have longevity."

Jim O'Sullivan asks, "Why am I going to die first?"

"Who cares!" responds Mario Bossi. "Let's drop the subject."

"You're a follower like the rest of us – plus you have some serious heath issues – you've been hospitalized more then anyone else," answers Mike Chitkowski.

"Speaking of hospital – which one would you like to visit?" yelled a ticked off electrician, who has to be held back from punching Mike.

"The president is important to this group. He's our leader and says he'll resign – but doesn't. He keeps us together and helps us through life's little problems." The treasurer continues, "If you look at people who have longevity, they had a purpose in life. They get up everyday because they were needed by someone else to function – live."

"What the hell is wrong with you?" asks Benny Benson.

"I think I'm going to cry," says an emotional president. He has a point, "If it weren't for me you screwballs wouldn't be close rich friends."

"Screw you – you hate being president"– hollers Jim O'Sullivan.

The treasurer continues, "If one of us dies he won't allow another person into F.I.C, we're one of a kind. The Kiss of Death Curse occurs because we're all linked together – the president knows this."

"We would find another stupid person to take your place," cites Benny Benson.

"No you won't, the president wouldn't let you. Things that happen to us will never happen to others. It's because of the president and the way he takes care of business which is why we didn't all disband and continue to lose money."

Again he's right. Trevor Goodman is now standing, walking around the room with his head held up high with a silly grin on he's face speaking to everyone. "I live to be President it's what keeps me alive. It's on the top of my list – above family and work. I'm glad that one of you jerks realizes how important the presidency is to me. It would be devastating to see one of you die,especially Mike."

He continues, "I've made a few mistakes, but overall I led with compassion and kindness never before seen in a leader – even through good and bad times. I never miss used my power. If one of you passed away then that would be the end of F.I.C."

Gary Glenn speaks, "I think you should resign."

The president drinks another ice beer, then adds, "The sadness felt by your families. what a nightmare it would be for me and them." (Fakes choking up.)

The Super bowl ended and before everyone went home, Trevor Goodman suggested he talk with the CFO privately about the situation – everyone is intoxicated to clearly discuss F.I.C's options.

The meeting lasted only a half an hour, but the CFO answered the President's questions exactly the way the President thought he would. The firm didn't care about F.I.C's relatives. The CFO suggests that F.I.C members ignore the problem they're not the only people suffering because of F.I.C. Plus F.I.C has a lot of money in its account because of the firm's offer.

"What if one member dies, would the offer continue with a new person on board?" asks Trevor Goodman.

"Is somebody going to die?" asks the CFO.

"No," answers the president. "I just thought I ask while it was on my mind."

"I don't know the answer to that," the CFO answers quickly.

"If F.I.C joins another firm, only to return to them – will the offer be rescinded? "

"Of course it would", states the CFO. "You think another firm would believe you're the Kiss of Death and offer you the same deal?"

"I don't know."

"Yes you do," says the CFO.

The President relays the answers to questions at the next meeting. The meeting was subdued and the members of F.I.C were ticked off at the firm's stance – they don't care about our families losing money – they actually said that! They also said to think about the large amounts of money in our account, responds Mike Chitkowski.

F.I.C selects Harley Davison Motorcycles (HDM) from the firms list. HDM sales have been climbing up the charts and they are expanding by the purchase of Shining Chrome – a company that supplied HDM with all of its chrome parts.

Within a year's time the company employees go on strike – demanding the same benefits received by the workers at Shining Chrome. The strike is planed for the spring - the company's biggest season for sales and parts. The price of HDM drops drastically. The Kiss of Death Curse continues – this time without affecting anyone's relatives.

The strike is settled within three months and the price of HDM starts to rebound. More money is deposited into F.I.C's account.

Two people, separate programs, both optimistic their version would be a hit, yet only one will be recognized as a pioneer in the field of investing. The programs paralleled each other, using "indicators" and "alerts", information would "pop up' on the online investor's computer screen to assist the investor to purchase or sell a particular stock.

Mike Chitkowski spoke to Jim Frond only twice last month, but phoned him several times recently to congratulate him on promoting his program nationally by using radio and T.V. appearances. Jim mentioned both media events were driving the sales and circulation of his computerized program across the country. The conversation then took a dramatic turn.

Mike admitted to Jim Frond, he figured out exactly what "indicators" and "alerts' he used as variables to decipher out certain stocks for failure. Before Jim thinks about a lawsuit and making false acknowledgements towards the treasurer, who is thinking about producing exactly the same program with improvements, Mike recommends they meet ASAP. He is interested in forming a partnership, and will divulge the variables that changes Jim's program into his, allowing investment strategists to focus on a higher level of "alerts" that will warn them of a near market crash or worse.

As the Treasurer of Futures Investment Club, he's used his computer program to predict the failure of several stocks over the last several months, allowing the investment club to benefit financially from his expertise. Jim agrees to meet with Mike Chitkowski privately.

As a student who worked hard in high school, yet didn't do well, Mike Chitkowski was motivated and confident he had the intelligence to figure out Jim Frond's complex system. He believed in himself has he made connection after connection with the same variables used by the experienced innovator. The brain was expanding, growing, learning, he wasn't stupid, just lazy.

Mike Chitkowski wasn't willing to spend the time, effort, or the money on his project. A partnership would be the easiest route to take. Why shouldn't he pressure Jim Frond to get things moving, the lawyers were taking to long with finalizing the agreement – but he was told to stop the frequent phone calls or the partnership will be rejected.

The Treasurer can't wait much longer. He wants to tell Susan how intelligent he really is, and how proud she would be of his accomplishments. The money, fame, and spotlight will shine on them as a couple, the future looks bright.

The CFO supplies F.I.C with the names of the five remaining stocks to choose from; United Tech, General Electric, Stanley Tool, Disney and McDonald's. Expect for McDonald's and Disney, all were solid Connecticut companies that have proven records since they were first established.

The members of F.I.C decided to vote on purchasing 100 shares of Stanley Tool at $23 a share and United Tech at $29 a share. Stanley Tool was located in the Polish section of New Britain CT., which hired many Polish immigrants. F.I.C renamed Stanley Tool calling it Sta-chu tool. Sta –chu tool payed a dividend of $21 quarterly and went up and down within a 10 dollar price range for the first three months F.I.C owed it. (Mostly up $10).

It was Trevor Goodman who announced he was attending the annual stockholders meeting this month for Sta - Chu tool, any one interested.

"Is there any food at these meetings?" asked Gary Glenn.

"Yes, lots of finger foods and alcohol," answers the President.

"Count me in," says Gary Glenn.

"Is the meeting going to be in New Britain, Ct.?" asks the Treasurer.

"No, in Poland," answers Benny Benson.

"Yes, it's always at the company's headquarters in New Britain, Ct." states the President.

"I'll go," answers Mike Chitkowski. Followed by, "I hope there are some Polish broads attending."

The three F.I.C members arrived early, and within seconds, Gary Glenn was in the food line sampling the hord'vers, while the treasurer checked out the females. Trevor Goodman quickly picked up on a conversation between two company employees standing next to the greeting table. They seemed agitated about the announce-ment today by their union regarding the layoffs. This also concerned the President, and he approached the two gentlemen to ask them for more details.

They informed Trevor Goodman the State of CT. was threatening withholding tax breaks offered to Stanley Tool because the company was going over seas to open a new factory – and hiring foreign workers. This process would involve the layoffs of newly hired personal at the main factory.

Tonight's meeting, covered by several local T.V. stations, would allow the company to answer questions regarding their decision to go over seas and lay off people. The Governor of Ct. and the mayor of New Britain attended the meeting.

The President pulled the Secretary away from the buffet table and found the Treasurer next to some Polish-speaking ladies, and the three took seats located in the middle of the room. After about an hour of heated exchanges between company officials and their employees, the President of Stanley Tool announced at the end of this year, the company will relocate part of its tool division to China and layoff the workers here in a cost saving measure. This was the first time that Stanley Tool ever had to layoff personal due to cheaper labor outside the U.S.A. – the most difficult decision The President of Stanley tool regretted, but needed doing.

"Thank god we didn't spend our own money on shares of Sta -Chu Tool, because tomorrow everyone owning it will start to sell off his or her shares," exclaimed Mike Chitkowski.

The price of Stanley Tool shares dropped $2 a share the next day, followed by another drop of $1 a share the following day.

Susan said she's owned the stock for over 5 years without it ever dropping more then $.25 a share.

Within one month of United Tech shareholders meeting, F.I.C members hear and see on T.V. two helicopter crashes involving United Tech engines in Iraq. Ten U.S. soldiers were killed due to engine failure. It was also announced on T.V., that the U.S. government engine contracts with Gen Electric and United Tech were up for renewals. This incident will be the deciding factor in which company the government will choose.

The government selects Gen Electric to a new five-year contract. The Curse continues.

Two hundred shares of McDonalds were bought for a price of $12 a share. It took six months of owning McDonald's, which reached as high as $29 a share (providing customers free coffee and a healthier menu), before the stock became the next victim on the Kiss of Death hit list. The cooking oil used by McDonald's was investigated and determined by the U.S. health and safety committee as containing dangerously high levels of fat in their French fries. Lawsuits were filed by overweight customers claiming McDonald's French fries caused their obesity. Also, a spread of mad cow disease in Europe affected their sale of hamburgers. McDonald's stock price drops to $9 a share.

Fifty shares of Disney World were purchased by F.I.C at $19 a share. The price of Disney climbs to $23 a share with the acquisition of ESPN sports Network in Bristol, Ct.

Then disaster hits the Disney parks in California and Florida with a series of terrorist threats, closing the parks down for six months. The price of Disney stock drops to $10 a share. More money is deposited into F.I.C's account. F.I.C's current assets are $60,000 – an average growth of $10,000 a year.

The assistant's office came with a private bathroom and doubled in size from her previous office - how embarrassing! Susan is out to prove to everyone in the firm that she deserves what she's been given.

The training sessions provided her with a smooth transition, but didn't include the CFO, who seemed to spend a lot of time behind closed doors. The only communication between them was two E-mails and three phone calls – nothing personal. Three days secluded in his office and finally he requests her presence.

His office wasn't much larger than hers, but included a wet bar, and a three person couch with matching end tables. He offers Susan a drink at 11am in the morning. She declines. Her addiction to alcohol and drugs, specifically crack, put her in rehab for two years and destroyed a marriage. Drinking at work would raise red flags. The CFO drinks a gin and tonic.

"I'm leaving the firm soon, and would like you to come with me. It's an Diverse Investment's office in Mass., and my nephew is working on a project that needs our assistance.

I can't go into the details at this time, but it involves people you know."

"This afternoon, representatives from the main office are coming to discuss major changes in our mutual fund portfolios. You need to take notes and make sure they don't touch our Growth Fund, pointing to a folder on his desk. If they tamper with it call me on my cell phone immediately."

The CFO walks over to Susan, gives her a big hug on being promoted and tells her on his way out the door – she's the hottest assistant Diverse Investment's has ever had while swallowing a second gin and tonic.

Susan picks up the folder, looks at the office clock, and sees she has about two hours to examine the information before the representatives start to appear. She returns to her office when the phone rings. The CFO tells Susan to give the brown briefcase located under his desk, to any of the representatives before they leave – he forgot to mention it to her.

The after noon meeting went smoothly, no problems. Susan handled the Growth Fund debate with professional ease, using the CFO notes to challenge any changes in question. Things went so well, she forgot about the CFO's surprising statement;"a project dealing with people she knew." The gentleman receiving the briefcase asked if he can take an extra week to return it. Susan said he'd have to talk to the CFO. He looked surprised when Susan couldn't give him the answer.

The members of F.I.C were informed of the meeting right after the profits from Disney were placed in the account by Susan. The CFO of the company is leaving and Susan was going with him to another firm – because of this change - they wanted to meet with F.I.C one last time.

They finished by saying how the six years of working together went by fast and wished F.I.C members continued success in the future. Everyone benefited financially by the Kiss of Death Curse.

The end of the ride, the stock market could breath a sigh of relief, the Kiss of Death Curse has ended.

The members of F.I.C decide to disband after meeting several times with the new CFO, who forbid any food or ice beer in the conference room and demanded F.I.C increase membership as well as dues. The members didn't like the changes she enforced – plus she was ugly. The new broker tried to talk F.I.C out of disbanding, but it was time for a reunion and the members of F.I.C wanted a reunion –so they decided to pack it in.

Mike Chitkowski receives a phone message from Jim Frond, "The lawyers have agreed on a partnership." Mike's excitement brings on a huge anxiety attack. The second part of the message produces more anxiety. "However, a third party is now involved, your lawyer as been contacted regarding a meeting with all parties."

PART 3

THE CAUSE OF THE CURSE

After several years together, the members of F.I.C are going their separate ways, but the question still remains - What caused the curse to exist? Is it worth the time and effort to investigate the Cause? Does anybody except the President of F.I.C think a curse actually existed?

Was it the actions of the group or did it happen because of someone within the group? The President of F.I.C needed to find out.

After a few months of separation, Trevor Goodman decides to call each F.I.C member to find out if they are still actively playing the stock market. He makes a calculated decision to lie to everyone and say he owns a few stocks. The members were told he is calling to investigate the reasons for the curse, which they all agree is a waste of time – what possible evidence could be found?

The only member to admit he's still involved in the stock market was Mike Chitkowski. When questioned about his stock selections, the treasurer explained his ownership of stocks was now a private matter. Mike always trusted the president, why the secrecy?

Trevor waited a few weeks, and then contacted Mike again by phone, using the topic of planning F.I.C's first reunion to bait him into divulging his stock picks. The treasurer reminds the president that it's all on his shoulders, no body is going to help organize a reunion and he doesn't have time to offer. Trevor understands and tells Mike he purchased two Exchange Traded Funds for his stock portfolio. "How about him, buying anything good?"

Mike Chitkowski didn't own any stocks, and he agreed with Jim Frond not to discuss the possible merger of programs until they meet. He doesn't know what to say to the president.

"Are your stocks failing?" questioned Mike.

"No. My two Exchange Traded Funds are doing fine," Trevor Goodman is lying again.

"What are Exchange Traded Funds?" asks the Treasurer.

The president is trying to remember all of the details about Exchange Traded Funds he recently read about in Money Magazine and why the article said they would be the future investment vehicles for people in the market. He's not a good liar. It takes a few minutes for him to remember the information but his memory comes back.

"Basically they're like a mutual fund, only they offer more flexibility than a mutual fund, because they trade through out the day like a stock, and investors can buy as little as a single share."

Mike Chitkowski starts asking several questions: 1.How many ETF's are there? Answer – hundreds – he's lying again. 2. How many shares did you buy? A hundred shares of each, another lie. 3. Did you pay a brokers fee? Yes. He's guessing they're fees involved. What are the names of the-------? The question never completed, because the president cleverly changes the topic and asks the treasurer what stocks he owns.

Trevor Goodman promises not to tell anyone, it's between you and me, trust me. He's lying again, and knows the treasurer will probably never forgive him when he finds out, but his obsession with finding the cause of the curse is over riding the loyalty of a friend.

A person, who hates liars and thieves, decides to place himself into the first category. Mike Chitkowski lies to the president, naming McDonalds and Disney as his two stocks.

A surprised president asks how long the treasurer owned them.

"Now you know, and remember it's between you and me" – states Mike Chitkowski without answering the follow up question, which would require another lie. "Good luck with the reunion and I have to get off the phone."

Two stocks owned by the treasurer, all of which failed under the ownership of F.I.C, interesting thought the president. He needed to read the money magazine article again, which listed twenty ETF funds, to get the names of two Exchange Traded Funds, keeping his lie alive.

The magazine was found and Trevor Goodman selects the names of two ETF funds from the list, and then calls Mike, leaving the names on his answering machine. He also calls Gary Glenn and Jim O'Sullivan to inform them of the stocks owned by the treasurer and his obsession with finding the cause of the curse.

They never had a reason to doubt his honesty, but the deceit is shocking. Trevor begs Jim and Gary not to tell Mike he disclosed the names to them. They don't trust him any more. They jokingly suggest the president go for counseling.

The new broker was happy to see the president again and wanted to know how he could help him with ETF funds.

After telling the broker he owned two ETF funds, Malaysia (EMM) and Australia (EMA) Index funds, Trevor Goodman asks if the firm has any recommendations. The broker names the ETF funds recommended by the firm, adding the two ETF funds you own are not rated by the firm. Look over the list and let me know which ones you are interested in buying.

"By the way, Mike Chitkowski is also interested in ETF funds. You should send him the same list."

"Thanks. I'll do that," responds the broker. "Can I call you at the end of the week?"

"Make it two weeks," says Trevor Goodman.

He's lied to the treasurer several times and the broker once. It's getting easier to lie. He does need help.

Trevor Goodman then carefully re -examines the minutes of every F.I.C meeting – maybe he can detect a pattern or find a clue. This process was going to take time – but he needed to know. As he patiently examined the paper work, certain events stood out.

In another calculated move, Trevor Goodman called the broker to get a second opinion on ETF's and asked if Mike Chitkowski put his order in yet?

"Yes, he purchased 100 shares of EMA and EMM, right after we initially talked. I recommend you dropping both ETFs, since the stocks are being negatively affected by the foreign market, without the chance of them rebounding soon. Unfortunately, Bob purchased the ETF's at a bad time."

He continues, "The firm is recommending the following ETF's, which are pricey right now – but solid investments."

"They're a little over my price range," responds Trevor Goodman. Then adds, "I wish I had the money to purchase some blue chip stocks Mike bought a while back, they've almost doubled in price."

"Do you know the names and time he purchased them?" asks the broker.

"Can't you look up his file and find out?" asks a confused president.

"He must have purchased them through another broker, the only stocks I'm handling is his ETF's. Have him call me with the names."

"I'll do that," promised Trevor Goodman.

Didn't Mike say he was using the firm and the new broker, or did Trevor Goodman assume he did?

The next step in the investigative process was to talk with Susan and the CFO.

"Susan, did the CFO show you the list of blue chip stocks before he offered them to F.I.C?"

"He never showed me the names."

"Did you ever question him about the offer?"

"What do you mean?"

"Why did he do it? Was it because of his belief in the curse or some other logical reason?"

"I don't think he believed in a curse as much as short selling. He read a lot of articles on short selling and kept saying the current market is vulnerable to drastic drops in volume, especially with blue chip stocks. He was constantly on the computer checking stocks."

"So he used the computer to create the list."

"Yes."

"Thanks for your time."

The location of the first reunion was at Benny Benson's fitness club. Trevor Goodman held the position of aquatic director and the members of F.I.C enjoyed the facility's tennis courts, swimming pool, and weight room as guests of Benny and the president. It's been one year since F.I.C disbanded and the president was worried that the guests might be to drunk to enjoy the place, but they managed to handle the situation.

Everything that happened to F.I.C, from the first meeting to the last was dissected and discussed at great lengths. It was amazing how many events were recalled in detail in only a few hours. F.I.C enjoyed a lot of good times together and because of the curse – profited. The reunion was about to end when Trevor Goodman asked the members, "What do they think caused the curse?"

"Who cares?" answered Mike Chitkowski.

Both Gary Glenn and Jim O'Sullivan respond, "We don't." Everyone else agrees - they don't care about the curse - only about the next reunion.

The second reunion was scheduled three years after the first, a golf vacation in Myrtle Beach. Everybody played golf and no one ever visited South Carolina, and since Mike Chitkowski's brother owned a timeshare that was available for only a small fee, the members decided to book the place for an April trip. The treasurer did a tremendous job of organizing the trip. He took care of the airline tickets, airport parking, rental car, and scheduled rounds of golf at various courses.

As the members of F.I.C waited for their luggage and clubs at the baggage terminal – the trip started to fall apart. The luggage and clubs didn't arrive with the F.I.C members. The airline person told F.I.C members that everything will arrive with the next scheduled flight, an hour from now. "No problem," says the President, "we'll be at the bar and pick them up in an hour."

The next flight arrived exactly on time, producing the entire luggage, but no golf clubs. The members were drunk and not happy. Benny Benson starts to swear at Mike Chitkowski for screwing up the plans. Everyone is looking at Trevor Goodman to solve the problem, when the airline person explains the clubs were intentionally left off the flight, because the plane was over loaded. The president tells the airline person the plane isn't the only thing that's overloaded – directing her attention to the drunken members of F.I.C. He then gives the airline person the phone and address of the resort, telling her that," If the clubs don't show up by 6am tomorrow, the airline is going to be buying a lot of golf equipment." The clubs arrived exactly at 6am the next day. Unfortunately, so did the tornado.

With a starting time of seven am, the members of F.I.C realize they might have to reschedule their tee times for later in the day, if the courses they were scheduled to play on were affected by the storm. They were. Tornado sirens were sounding alarms all night long and the winds were bending trees outside their time share condo. The tee times were for courses located across the street, which took a direct hit from the tornado, and were unplayable. After calling their wives to let them know they were still alive, they traveled ten miles to play golf on another course.

Day two provided a great day of golf and no problems. An evening trip to the driving range however, created an unbelievable situation.

Everyone hopes and prays they die peacefully and without suffering. No one knows when the end will come. People die in their homes, traveling, in accidents, at work, and during reunions.

The other members of F.I.C wished it didn't happen on a golf vacation and without his family present, but it probably was best they weren't around to see him "kick the bucket."

He passed away sitting next to the ball machine at the Myrtle Beach C.C. driving range. No one noticed him until he accidentally kicked a bucket of balls while collapsing on the floor next to the machine. This happened immediately following the electrical shock that sent large amounts of electricity through Steve's weak heart. Steve's hand got stuck in the opening of the machine when he tried to assist the machine in giving him the correct number of balls. His sweaty hands and the electrical contacts he touched sent 220 volts of electricity into his body.

Steve Culcarta's burnt hand was bandaged by management and the members of F.I.C. did the best they could with CPR, but he succumbed to heart failure arriving at the hospital.

The members of F.I.C are gathered outside the funeral home, not knowing what to say to each other, when Mike Chitkowski speaks.

"Are we going to have another reunion?" Pause – no one answers. The treasurer continues, "up until the time of his unexpected death, everyone was having a great time. I like to see us put this tragedy behind us and plan another reunion."

"This isn't a good time to discuss the next reunion," says Trevor Goodman.

Benny Benson turns to the Treasurer, "I wish you took the dirt nap instead of him."

Jim O'Sullivan adds," you were wrong, I didn't die first", directing his anger at the treasurer.

It took just a few seconds for everyone to remember "the order of death" predicted by Mike Chitkowski.

About three years following the death of Steve Culcarta, the treasurer phones Trevor Goodman to offer organizing the next reunion, unless he feel's it's to soon after Steve's death? The president thinks the members are ready to meet again – what do you have in mind?

"The location is going to be a surprise," answers Mike Chitkowski. Then ads, "How are your stocks doing?"

"I sold both stocks," again lying to the treasurer. "I think I'm the curse- my stocks tanked soon after I bought them. Are your stocks doing o.k.?"

"Yes they are," revealed Mike. I'm grateful for your tip on the ETF stocks. They're starting to rebound. I'm surprised you didn't hold on to them."

Trevor Goodman asks, "How's McDonalds and Disney doing?"

"I lied to you. I don't own either stock," admits the treasurer. A surprised president hears Mike tell him he knows his lying too.

Trevor Goodman wondered, "How did you find out?"

"Gary and Jim told me just before the first reunion," says the treasurer. "Let's come clean and stop the lies – the Kiss of Death Curse happened because of us – you and me."

"Prove it," ordered Trevor Goodman, who plans on calling the two jerks to thank them for keeping a secret.

"You don't own any ETF stock and I never personally owned Disney or McDonalds. I decided to purchase the EFT stocks you recommended and what happens to them? They fail but later rebound into solid investments. Every time F.I.C received the CFO's list, you or I pushed the purchasing of a certain stock, without any other member challenging us. Whatever we did they followed. Check the minutes of the meetings, the curse happened because of actions we took."

Mike was right. The minutes reflected the votes towards stocks the treasurer and he strongly recommended. However, the final stock selected to fail was always the stock Mike persuaded F.I.C to pick. Plus, the treasurer purchased the two ETF stocks on his own and they failed, continuing the curse beyond the investment clubs involvement. The president is starting to point the finger at the treasurer as the cause of the curse.

"What really concerns me is that the Kiss of Death curse we hold is taking on a new meaning."

Trevor Goodman asks, "What are you taking about?"

"We plan the reunions and already some one has died because of our actions. I'm worried about the next reunion, and the possibility of someone else dying."

Except for the first reunion, the treasurer planned the second and wants to plan the third reunion, why did he say they planned the reunions – it was he and he's worried about someone else dying?

"That's ridiculous, plan the reunion. The other members aren't concerned about dying at the next reunion, only partying," replies Trevor Goodman.

Susan doesn't answer the phone, because the caller ID identifies the caller. He leaves a strange message on her voice mail. "Thanks for introducing me to "Strategies for Success" my life is about to change drastically. I would like you to attend F.I.C's next reunion. I hope you call me back. I want you to be happier than anyone else."

Susan can't understand why he would call her and chance losing the partnership. Maybe he thinks she doesn't know? Susan decides not to inform the CFO about the call. The guy deserves a chance to succeed. But she's also concerned about him wanting her to be happy!

The members of F.I.C are headed to the secret location for reunion #3. Jim O'Sullivan is driving a huge extended cap pick up truck he borrowed from the electrical company and the passengers are drinking "ice beer" while trying to figure out were they're going.

Jim O'Sullivan and his passengers would have recognized the area had the treasurer taken the old route to the cottage. Instead he tells the driver to follow route 85, completed just a month ago, which brings travelers to the lake from the Mass. side. They will pass the famous bar, which is now an upscale martini bar, and stop at the next stop sign, allowing the members to look directly across the lake to see the cottage.

At the stop sign, Jim asks Mike Chitkowski, "Which way? Straight or left?"

Mike answers by telling the driver and passengers that they have arrived at the secret location, "Does anything look familiar?"

The larger lake was to their left and if they went straight ahead would drive over a road that separated one lake from the other by a bridge. Mario Bossi now remembers, because he caught a large fish casting into the smaller lake from the other side of the bridge. He can't believe his eyes, the cottage was repainted, but the storm wall was still in tack.

The other passengers start to realize where they are and can't believe the treasurer brought them back to Steve Culcarta's cottage so soon after his death. What was he thinking about?

The passengers are looking at Mike, and the treasurer says there's another surprise waiting for them at the cottage.

"Let me guess, you dug up his body, and he's waiting for us at the front steps," says Benny Benson.

The treasurer answers, "Close – a very close guess."

"This is freaking me out," says Gary Glenn. "I have a bad feeling about this location."

Benny Benson is looking at the president, "Did you agree with Mike about having the reunion here?"

"No, I had no idea," responds the president.

Jim O'Sullivan says, "I have a bad feeling about us partying here." (So does the president)

"Drive up to the cottage, there's another surprise waiting for us," insisted Mike Chitkowski.

"This is bad luck. You should have told us about the cottage," exclaimed Trevor Goodman.

"It wouldn't have been a surprise, and there's another surprise waiting for us," repeats the treasurer.

Benny Benson declares, "We're so happy about the first surprise that you want us to be ticked off about another?"

"You're going to enjoy the next surprise, I guarantee you," responds Mike Chikowski.

The pickup truck proceeds up the driveway and parks in front of the cottage, where two people are sitting on the steps.

"Holy Shit! I can't believe my eyes!" Exclaims Benny Benson upon seeing the CFO and Susan sitting on the steps waving to everyone in the truck, "Why did you invite them?"

Gary Glenn asks, "Why not?"

"Hey, I'm glad he did," added Jim O'Sullivan.

"Me too," states Trevor Goodman.

Mike Chitkowski didn't invite both of them and he's not happy.

The truck is unloaded and everyone heads back to the patio to have a vodka and coke in a Shell Gas Station cup, as a tribute to Steve Culcarta. While several more drinks were consumed, the treasurer finalized the agenda.

Susan immediately announces to a shocked treasurer and the members of F.I.C that she's engaged to the CFO. If looks could kill, everyone noticed Mike Chitkowski's face turn red with anger. Susan explains their both here to share the celebration with the members of F.I.C. She remembered the stories about the famous bar across the lake and told the CFO about it. They would like to treat the members of F.I.C to dinner and drinks at the bar, which is now an upscale martini bar name the Olive Garden.

"I don't drink martinis," announced Mike Chitkowski in a defiant voice.

"We do!" shouts Benny Benson.

"I hope you brought a million dollars with you, because once we start drinking and eating it's going to cost you an arm and a leg," mentions Trevor Goodman.

"It's the least we can do to thank you for supplying us with predicted wealth," answered the CFO.

"That's true, and I'm hungry. Let's go celebrate," says Gary Glenn.

The treasurer isn't getting any of the credit and he's holding back because of the agreement.

The martini bar was filed with young people, drinking different types of martinis, while eating expensive foods from the menu. The tab for the evening was very high, because the members of F.I.C were ordering up and down the menu, downing martinis like they were water. When the bill came, the CFO and Susan quickly told the waiter and everyone else, they would pay the entire cost, including the tip. Everyone was glad Mike invited the CFO and Susan.

Sitting next to F.I.C's table were six young adults, three males and three females, all dressed up as if they were headed to a wedding. One of the males leans over to Mike Chitkowski and asks him, "Was the investment club successful?"

Surprised by the question, but aware that F.I.C members tend to be loud when intoxicated, he assumes the guy over heard some table conversations and answers by saying "yes", followed by, "Thanks to the curse."

My God, he doesn't recognize me. They were never officially introduced, but he saw him several times across the hall, talking to Jim Frond. The full beard on his face and lose of several pounds recently confused friends of his who haven't seen him in a few months, yet he didn't even recognize his voice. He must be drunk. The young man asked Mike Chitkowski to repeat what he just said, checking once again to see if his voice sounded familiar to the treasurer.

"You heard me correctly (speaking in a slurred speech pattern), we had this curse that affected the stock market and we profited over the outcomes. We were successful at selecting blue chip stocks." Mike Chitkowski made these statements to the guy while downing his fifth martini.

The young man knew a lot of martinis were consumed, but the treasurer wasn't making any sense. "What was the name of your club?"

"Futures Investment Club," answered the treasurer.

The young man wrote the name down on his napkin, and glanced over Mike Chitkowski's shoulder to see the lone female at the table. She looked very familiar.

When he first saw her she was identified as a client of his, then her visits became more regular, always carrying a brief case into his boss's office. What was she trying to sell?

Then he sees her sitting with the members of F.I.C, and recognizes her again, yet she doesn't know it's him. During the celebration, she leaves the table to enter the rest room, but pauses a few seconds near the bar, where his boss was standing having a drink. This was the darkest area of the barroom, and if someone didn't snap a picture exactly as they passed, he never would have witness them exchange kisses in the dark.

Someone did mention the possibility of F.I.C getting back together, but for some reason the thought wasn't taken seriously. There was no mention of the Kiss of Death Curse during the entire celebration.

In the future, the members of F.I.C promised to invite the CFO and Susan to every reunion – as long as they continue to pay the bar tap. Trevor Goodman will call them regarding the next reunion.

Everyone left the bar together, the members of F.I.C in the truck headed back to the cottage to spend the night, while Susan and the CFO headed north back to Massachusetts.

While reading the morning paper, Mike Chitkowski sees a small photo about an accident involving two cars on the Mass turnpike. The picture of the accident scene was horrible - no one survived the event. The names of the victims were withheld pending the notification of the relatives. He quickly throws the paper in the trash and awakens Trevor Goodman.

The doctor warned him to start exercising or change his life style. His cholesterol and weight rose to unacceptable levels. The doctor also suggested membership in a health club or purchase a treadmill for his house.

He buys an expensive treadmill over the cheaper ones because the deluxe models had two beer can holders and another opening for a sandwich. He placed the treadmill in front of his new H.D. T.V. and started to workout every day.

By the end of the first week, he felt lousy. He had severe pains in his lower back and couldn't sleep. With a flight scheduled for tomorrow to Dubai, he was trying to decide if he should check with a doctor. He decides the problem is with the treadmill. He exercised too much at high speeds. A weeks rest will do him good. His flight was smooth and scheduled to arrive in Dubai by six a.m. U.S. A. time.

The pain in his back was horrendous – he was having trouble breathing. The doctor on board determined he was having a serious medical emergency and alerted the flight crew the plane needed to land immediately. The flight crew decides to land in Saudi Arabia, the closest airport for emergency care, this will take another two hours. The doctor tries to give him fluids, but he starts to go in and out of consciousness. By the time the plane lands, his blood has become toxic, the emergency was worse than the doctor on board diagnosed. His days as a traveling salesman are over. The company flies Gary Glenn's body back to the U.S.A.

The members of F.I.C are gathered outside the funeral parking lot, not knowing what to say to each other, when Benny Benson speaks. "I thought you were going to call the CFO and Susan about the funeral."

"I did," answers the president. "But they couldn't make it."

"That's too bad; I was looking forward to seeing them again," says Benny Benson. Everyone is shaking their heads about the death of another F.I.C member. The members meet their wives at the cars and drive home.

Later that night, the treasurer calls the president. "Why did you lie to the rest of the members about the CFO and Susan?"

"Why didn't you jump in to tell them the truth," responds Trevor Goodman?

"For the same reasons you didn't, the Kiss of Death Curse," exclaims Mike Chitkowski.

"Exactly," says Trevor Goodman. "I can't sleep any-more."

Mike Chitkowski asks, "What are we going to do?"

"Where not having any more reunions, that's for sure. Start thinking about an explanation, because I can't," requests the president.

It took only a couple of days following the funeral, when Benny Benson calls the president to ask for the CFO and Susan's phone number.

"Why do you need to talk to them," asks Trevor Goodman?

"It's none of your business," answers Benny Benson. "I'm only kidding, they mentioned this Diverse Investment's' annuity they wanted me to invest in, and I want to discuss it with them."

The President gives the phone number to Benny and notifies Mike Chitkowski.

A week later, the call comes in from the Benny Benson. "They couldn't make it (long pause) – at least you didn't lie. Was it in the Connecticut papers?" asks Benny.

"I don't think so," says Trevor Goodman. "Have you told anybody else?"

"Everyone knows. Another reunion and two more people die."

"I'm afraid so."

"You were right – Mike holds the curse – let's kill him before he continues to kill us."

"I can't sleep anymore thinking about it. Does everyone feel the same way?" asks Trevor.

"About killing him, no that's my suggestion. All agree he's the curse and not you. I'll be glad to tell him how we all feel. Did you see the look on his face when they announced they were engaged?"

"Yes I did," answered the president.

"Do you think he killed them because of Susan?"

"Jesus no!" exclaims the president. "He was with one of us every minute of the reunion."

Benny Benson asks, "Are you sure you don't want me to tell him everyone thinks he's the curse?"

"Yes I'm sure. I'll tell him."

"You're the one they say carries the curse. You need to prove to them they're wrong," explains Trevor Goodman.

"The accident was just that – an accident. The other death was due to his failing business. The secretary's death was his own fault, so how I'm I the curse?" asks Mike.

"Benny thinks you killed them because of Susan. You said the curse had taken on a different meaning and everybody else agrees."

"I don't hold the curse – we hold the curse."

"They think it's you, and only you."

Mike Chitkowski asks, "You think people are dying because of me?"

"I don't know what to think anymore. Gary's death was only two weeks after the last reunion you planned but I think I have an idea that can help you."

"I don't need any help. They're the ones who need help. (Pause) What's your plan?"

"It's not finalized in my mine yet, but it's going to take a couple of weeks to set in motion, and unfortunately, you can't know the entire plan or it will fail."

"Then what?" asks the treasurer.

"Plan B kicks in, which includes Benny killing you before the next reunion."

"Very funny, am I supposed to laugh now or later? A couple of weeks are all you have because I'm going to call everyone up and tell them to shove the curse up their rear ends."

Trevor Goodman wishes he actually had a plan A. Again he's lying to Mike and he's concerned about the deaths of Steve Culcarta, Gary Glenn, the CFO and Susan.

PART 4.

THE INVESTIGATION

The phone call came in about three months following F.I.C's third reunion at the cottage. It was from a person who claims introduced himself at the martini bar to the treasurer. He was sitting at the table next to F.I.C's and was able to track down details of F.I.C's involvement within the stock market. He needed to ask Trevor Goodman a couple of questions. The treasurer claimed F.I.C had a curse - that somehow rewarded F.I.C with profits. "Was that true? Second, why did the members of F.I.C stop meeting as an investment club if they were successful?"

Trevor Goodman asks the caller for more information about himself, and decides not to answer the questions without knowing who he really is?

"I understand." The caller identifies himself. "My name is Jack O'Brien, let's meet to discuss my interest in the answers. I'm heavily involved with the stock market and so are my associates who were at the bar with me. We have our own brokerage firm in Masssachusetts."

He agrees to meet with the caller next week, which will give him time to look over pictures taken by Mike

Chitkowski of the last reunion, hoping the photos show background images. Sure enough, several pictures show a group of young adults sitting next to F.I.C's table. One picture showed Susan kissing a person near the bar. This shot must have made Mike furious, thought the president.

The brokerage firm's lobby and front desk looked familiar and the conference room up on the higher level had an eerie feel to it, like Trevor Goodman used the room before.

The young man greets Trevor Goodman and they both move from the lobby to his office. Once inside, Jack O'Brien offered the president a drink. He then said how sorry he was to hear about the deaths of your friends following the reunion.

The young man knew a lot about that evening. Trevor Goodman asks, "How is it you know about the deaths?"

"Their pictures were in the papers, and I recognized them. Plus, in their obituaries they said a lot about them and their firm, Diverse Investment's. You know this is a Diverse Investment's office?"

"I thought things looked familiar," answers the president.

"So, tell me about the curse your associate told me about at the martini bar and your investment clubs successes within the stock market."

" Why is it so important for you to know the answers?"

"Because we have only one investment club and they are struggling. I thought you and your members might be able to offer some advice, and keep them moving forward, become as successful as your club. You were having a great time at the bar, and some of the stories I over heard seem familiar to the current club we have here."

Trevor Goodman questions Jack O'Brien, "Give me an example of a story you overheard."

"The one about the Club Golf IPO, how you wasted the profits at an off track racing pallor, our club did the same thing at a casino."

"How many in the club?" asks Trevor Goodman.

"The club is down from nine to four current members. They all like to drink beer and have a good time at the meetings. Only one member is really serious about the market, the others go with the flow. My associates and I have tried to offer suggestions, since they are losing money, but they won't listen. Their in the process of quitting - things are that bad."

"Sounds familiar," says the president. I think our treasurer is the perfect person to talk to them."

"Great, so tell me about the curse."

"You'll have to wait until he talks to the club to hear all the details." Trevor Goodman avoids talking about the curse. "Unfortunately, two key people involved with the investment club just died. I'm guessing the club won't want to meet with anyone, especially if they refused your help."

"I'm going to lie to them, and tell them you're offering to purchase the beer and snacks for the meeting if they agree to hear you speak. That should do it. The firm will cover the cost of everything. If the treasurer refuses to accept the invitation, will you be available to speak?"

"He'll be there. Make sure you purchase a few six packs of ice beer. What's the name of the investment club," asks Trevor Goodman?

"B.S.Club, and the letters do stand for bullshit," answers Jack O'Brien.

As the broker and the president walk back to the main lobby to say their good byes, they pass Jim Frond's office. Jack doesn't react to the screaming conversation Mr. Frond was having over the phone with Mike Chitkowski, but the screaming does get the attention of Trevor Goodman who looks into the office to catch a glimpse of the agitated person. Imagine if the president knew who was on the other line.

Jack stops in to brief Jim Frond about the meeting with the president of F.I.C. He informs his boss that everything went as planned.

"Did Trevor Goodman mention anything about his uncle (the CFO) or Susan when discussing the curse?"

"No, he didn't talk about the curse. He said the treasurer is coming with the president next week to discuss it."

"That should be interesting," exclaims Jim Frond

The accident will be reported as a finder bender, no one was seriously hurt. He called 911 because the driver of the other vehicle left the scene. The second officer to arrive on the scene didn't recognize him, but Jack recognized his roommate immediately. They spent nine months together at the State Police academy; training to become the academy's 305th graduating class.

The long double shifts, with little sleep, followed by lost weekends and holidays, kept him from continuing as a police officer. The bond between one officer to another, especially a partner, was the hardest part to leave behind, but he had family working in several brokerage firms, and could easily find employment.

Jack O'Brien was giving a uniformed police officer a key witness account of the accident, including license number and make of car, when detective Rich Casella recognized the voice.

"So you're back doing under cover work?"

"Special assignment."

"Whatever. Your beard makes you look five years older, but the weight loss was a good idea."

"Thanks. Congratulations on being promoted to detective. What brings you to the accident scene?"

"The car that took off is of interest to me."

"I understand. So how's the family doing?'

"Their doing great - I thought someone said you passed the brokers exam and were leaving the department."

"I have one more assignment to finish, and then I'm going to work at a firm in Peabody Mass."

"You and I should get together and reminisce about old times."

"That sounds like a great idea, but we seem to always have conflicting schedules. I'll call you next week and see if we can find the time." Jack O'Brien doubts they'll attempt to see each other.

On their way to the meeting, Mike Chitkowski asks Trevor Goodman if there's going to be another reunion.

The president asks, "What do you think?"

"I want you to have another reunion without me."

A stunned president asks the treasurer to repeat what he just said.

"I want you to plan it, but I don't want to attend the next reunion. The members of F.I.C. and you think that I'm the curse, so there's only one way to fine out if it's true."

"I can't do that," says Trevor Goodman.

"The members will be happy to hear I can't make the next reunion. You need to promise me that you and only you plan the reunion."

"This is crazy, this wouldn't prove a thing, let's think about this some more." In reality, that's just the idea the president had in his mine – plan A.

Trevor Goodman and Mike Chitkowski have reached their destination, and are walking into the lobby of the brokerage firm. The noise could be heard coming out of the conference room on the upper level of the first floor. Someone just finished telling a joke and the laughter spilled into the lobby, mixed in with sounds of beer cans opening.

Trevor Goodman and Mike Chitkowski looked at each other as if to say, "Are we at a F.I.C. meeting?"

Jack O'Brien noticed the president and treasurer standing in the lobby and asked them to wait while he notified the investment club that they have arrived. Mike Chitkowski recognizes Jack's voice and wonders why he looks so unfamiliar?

The investment club now wishes to meet the people who purchased the best beer they have ever tasted.

The conversations stopped when the two guests walked into the conference room. After introducing the president and treasurer of Futures Investment Club, Jack introduces the members sitting around the conference table. Then one of the members welcomes the guests by telling them to help themselves to beer and snacks. The ice beer was already gone.

"First, let me thank you for supplying the beer and food," says a member sitting at the head of the table, and then he says, "We need to know why you want to talk to us."

The members of B.S. were all in their late twenties, and most of them had a least three empty ice beer cans in front of them. Two members were dressed in shirt and ties, while the other two wore casual clothing.

"We're here to drink and learn some new jokes," answers Mike Chitkowski, trying to break the ice. No reaction.

"Actually, we might be able to answer questions about how we made $60,000 dollars in six years of meeting as an investment club," adds Trevor Goodman.

"That's an average of $10,000 dollars a year," says an excited obese member setting next to a smaller sized member, who adds "gee, you figured that out without a calculator".

The member sitting at the head of the table identifies himself has the President of B.S. and says ther're two things that interest us. One, "Your club was very successful at selecting blue chip stocks," and two "Why would a club disband after several successful years?"

Trevor Goodman and Mike Chitkowski were about to speak at the same time, when the treasurer lets the president speak.

"Actually, the last six years were the most successful, and knowing that most investment clubs shut down after two years, we some how managed to survive the initial years which included many membership changes and the stock crashes of 1987 and 2000."

"Thanks to the leadership of the president, we didn't give up, and kept plugging along until things started to fall in place," added Mike Chitkowski.

Jack O'Brien apologies for interrupting, but informs the guests that B.S. Club is in its third year of membership and collects $25 a month from each member. The cash balance in their account is only $200. Originally there were nine members of the B.S.Club, but they all cashed out.

"Tonight's meeting was arranged to vote on disbanding, but Jack said to wait until we talked to you. Again, please explain why you disbanded after several years of membership and how you made money purchasing blue chip stocks," asks the President of B.S...

"F.I.C had a great relationship with the firm, until the broker and CFO left. Then a new team was assigned to F.I.C and wanted to make drastic changes – like increasing membership and dues. We didn't want to change our ways, so we decided to disband rather then look for other brokerage firms." The first question answered by Trevor Goodman.

"If you allow us to return, we can specifically explain the steps we took in selecting blue chip stocks. It's not a simple answer," replies Mike Chitkowski to the next question without allowing the president to speak. Surprised by Mike's answer, Trevor Goodman didn't talk, but accepted the treasurer's response.

The obese member of B.S. talks," If you supply the ice beer and snacks again, I'm sure everyone else will be o.k. with meeting one more time..." Everyone else nods their heads, including Jack.

Mike Chitkowski informs Trevor Goodman that he needs to use the rest room before they leave, he'll be right back. He quickly walks down the main corridor to Jim Frond's office. He enters the office by stating his opposition again of delaying the partnership, due to the death of the CFO.

"Before he died you agreed to become a silent partner. Now you want his piece of the pie or the partnership is done. You can't have it your way, remember you came to me; I didn't seek you out," reaffirms Jim Frond.

Upon the return of the treasurer, Trevor Goodman mentions to Mike the restroom was right in front of him, he needs to get his eyes checked.

With the date set for three months from tonight's meeting, the ticked off treasurer and the president are driving home trying to figure out how to explain to B.S. that F.I.C wasn't exactly successful at picking blue chip stocks as they were picking the next "Kiss of Death victim".

Trevor Goodman is anxious to see if the curse continues with another club. "Can someone interested in destroying a company use the computer to hack into company information. Like e- mails?"

"A good hacker can get private information from anyone using a computer, what's on your mind?"

"I think the CFO was hacking into specific private e-mails or other internet information of a company to reduce the company's stock price. He some how obtained inside information."

"So you're telling me there was no curse, but a list of company stocks supplied by the CFO that he unlawfully obtained information from."

"Not only him, but you!"

In shock, Mike Chitkowski asks, "You think I'm a criminal?"

No answer from the president.

"I'm not a criminal. I would never use a computer unlawfully- never!"

Both men didn't speak to each other for several minutes until Trevor Goodman says he believes him and apologies.

Jack O'Brien meets with Jim Frond in his office. He believes the merger between the two clubs will happen. Using his photographic eye, he notices the brief case under Jim Frond's desk never moved since Susan's last visit, but a large four draw metal cabinet was missing. Jack needs to check with the surveillance team.

The remaining members of F.I.C were contacted about a meeting at the president's house concerning a new development regarding another investment club and the planning of F.I.C's next reunion.

Trevor Goodman and Mike Chitkowski discuss with the remaining members of F.I.C, the possibility of joining another investment club to create F.I.C II.

"Why would we want to do that?" asks Benny Benson.

"Because it's the ideal time to re-enter the stock market, the prices of blue chip stocks are at record discount prices, it's a buyers market. You can't win if you don't play," a lotto phrase used by Mike Chitkowski to emphasize his point.

"Why would we accept total strangers into our club," asks Jim O'Sullivan?

"Let's meet the members of BS club face to face and take it from there," recommends the President." You're going to be surprised at how similar they are to us."

The members of F.I.C decide to meet the members of BS club to discuss the merger.

A person contacts the Mass. State police to request they look into the connection with F.I.C and the deaths of two people they did business with. The person has some back round information about the investment club the detective might be interested in. Like the fact they disbanded as an investment club right after the two subjects stopped representing the club in some legally questionable stock transactions and were killed following a F.I.C reunion. Plus, there was a possible relationship between the Treasurer of F.I.C and the female victim.

The Massachusetts.State police assign newly appointed Det. Rich Casella to the case, (Nick- named Det. Colombo by his fellow officers, because of his investigative methods).

The names of the members of F.I.C were in the detective's hands, and he started to call each one to inform them of a request by an unknown source concerned about the accidental deaths of the CFO and broker. The list started with Steve Culcarta, followed by Benny Benson, Mike Chitkowski, Gary Glenn, Mario Bossi, Jim O'Sullivan, and Trevor Goodman.

The death of her husband was conveyed to the detective by his widow, who mentioned the death occurred during F.I.C's first reunion and is in a state of shock being questioned by a state trooper. "There shouldn't be any concern; I'm only doing this to satisfy an inquiry. I won't be calling again." She immediately contacts the President of F.I.C.

The answering machine said to call the police department at his convenience. Is this some kind of a sick joke wondered the Treasurer? He then contacts the President to find out if Benny Benson is screwing around with him.

The return call mentioned calling Mike Chitkowski – he might be a person of interest according to Benny Benson's return message. The detective should call him between these hours, so that he has plenty of time to talk about the accident, deaths, curse, and Mike who is probably the killer, since he planned both reunions and invited the CFO and broker to the third reunion. He also mentions the relationship the treasurer was trying to establish with the victim. He then contacts the President of F.I.C.

His wife said to answer the phone; it's a detective from the Mass. State police department. "Can you give me a number that I can confirm this is legit," asks Mario Bossi after calling the state police barracks. He's in shock that he is actually giving information to a real detective. He then contacts the President of F.I.C.

His cell phone rings, and his wife tells him to be home on time, so he won't miss his son's first varsity game, then mentions to call a detective at the following number. She's concerned about the reason for the call. "What do you think this is all about?" asks his wife.

"I have no idea," answers Jim O'Sullivan. After his short talk with the detective he calls the President of F.I.C.

The detective is told by Gary Glenn's wife her husband died while traveling abroad two weeks following a F.I.C reunion. The detective doesn't ask her any questions and tells her he won't be calling again.

Trevor Goodman expected a call, but it never happened. Instead the detective surprised him with a visit.

The introductions were done and Trevor Goodman offered the detective some thing to drink and said it was o.k. for him to smoke his cigar in the house. The president wondered why the detective didn't take his trench coat off in the house.

Trevor Goodman asked if he could ask a few questions before the detective asked his. "Certainly," answered the detective.

"Who started this inquiry?"

Detective Casella can't divulge the source at this time.

Second question,"What was the cause of the accident in Massachusetts?"

"Speed, alcohol, and possibly murder, the car's brakes are being examined" answers the detective.

"You're investigating a murder?"

"State forensic specialists are examining the car as we speak. The detective continues, "I have only one question to ask, "Do you believe there's any connection to the F.I.C reunions and the deaths of the Steve Culcarta, Gary Glenn, the CFO and Susan Weber?"

"No," answers a surprised Trevor Goodman.

"Did you or any member of F.I.C know anyone else in the martini bar?"

"Not that I'm aware of," answers the president while thinking about the detective asking him two questions while stating he was going to ask only one.

"Thank you for your time and I probably won't be contacting you again," says Det. Casella.

"That's it!" asks the president

"That's it," responds the detective.

The detective leaves and the President are just about to call the members of F.I.C, when the door bell rings.

"One more question before I leave," asks Det. Casella, "When is F.I.C's next reunion?"

"We're in the process of planning it," responds the president.

"Let me know when you do," asks the detective. "Here's my card."

The remaining members of F.I.C meet at the President's house to discuss the police investigation and the next reunion.

Everyone points the finger at Benny Benson, and Mike Chitkowski is furious that he would stoop to such a low level of accusation. Benny swears on the bible that he didn't contact the detective, and is going to have Det. Casella confirm the fact by calling his cell phone. The detective confirms the fact to all members, none of them made the inquiry. Then who called the state police, wonders the president? The member's of F.I.C are dumbfounded.

"What are we going to do?" asks Mario Bossi.

"If we have another reunion, I've been ask to report the date and location to the detective," says Trevor Goodman. He never mentions the part about a murder investigation.

"Your going to have another reunion without me," states Mike Chitkowski.

"You mean we're going to have all the remaining reunions without you," corrects Benny Benson.

"I don't want or need another reunion," says Jim O'Sullivan.

"You really mean that?" asks the president.

"Yes I do," answers Jim O'Sullivan.

"I want you to have another reunion without me, to prove to everyone, mostly the jerk seating in front of me (Benny Benson) that I'm not the curse."

"I agree with that request," says Benny Benson. "Let's put it to a vote, those in favor of having future reunions without the killer, I mean Mike, raise your hand." He's the only one that raises his hand.

Everyone can't believe Benny used the word killer, no one is laughing.

"We need to think about this situation a little more," says Trevor Goodman.

"You mean a little less!" wise cracks Benny Benson.

"Some one mentioned going to Block Island for a reunion. I think it was Gary who said he had a time share there we could use. I recommend we plan the next reunion there, without the killer," suggests Benny Benson.

"I didn't kill anyone, but I'm thinking about choking you!" shouts Mike Chitkowski

Trevor Goodman gets between both men to stop the attack..

"I'm calling the detective to inform him you just threaten me."

"I agree with Jim, we don't need anymore reunions," says Mario Bossi trying to reduce the tension between Mike and Benny.

Benny doesn't let up.

"We have to have another reunion to prove beyond a reasonable doubt that Mike is the killer."

"Wouldn't be ironic if you accidently fell off the ferry going over to Block Island, without me aboard," says the treasurer.

"Let's calm down, and decide what to do," remarks Trevor Goodman. Steve and Mario don't want anymore reunions, and I'm hesitating about having another, so that's three out of five who question the scheduling of a reunion."

Benny Benson says, "I'm not afraid of dying, and my chances of surviving another reunion is almost certain if Mike doesn't go."

An angered treasurer responds, "God is going to punish you for calling me a killer."

"That's it, then," says Mario Bossi, again trying to stop the tension between Mike and Benny. "No more reunions."

"No more reunions," says Jim O'Sullivan.

Trevor Goodman speaks, "I'll call the detective to inform him we're not having anymore reunions."

"I hope you're happy," says Benny Benson looking directly at the treasurer. "Please tell the detective he threaten to kill me."

The treasurer does go after Benny but is restrained by everyone else.

The phone call never got through, so the president left a message with the detective that there wasn't going to be anymore F.I.C reunions, inferring possibly that there was a connection to the reunions and the inquiry.

The condo was in a perfect location, within walking distance to Block Island beach's and restaurants. His family was going to enjoy a week on this active island before the invasion of summer tourist next week. The time share was expensive to rent, but the weather was predicted to be perfect and he and his family needed some quality family time away from relatives and friends. While checking in, the vacation started off to a great start, for Meredith the property manger welcomed Trevor Goodman with a surprise – you're staying rent free thanks to the Gary Glenn's wife who just sold the condo. The new owner had to pay the price of your rent (weekly maintenance fee) as part of getting the condo immediately and cheap. In fact, the new owner says he knows you and your family.

Trevor Goodman asks, "What's the person's name?"

Meredith gives him the name of Mike Chitkowski. Thank God Trevor Goodman's wife wasn't present to hear the answer. She hands over the deposit check, and wishes Trevor and his family a great week on the island. I wish I had friends like yours that would pay for my vacation.

He blamed the lack of sleep on the noise created by planes flying over the condo, which were landing at the island's airport. The president was going to call the treasurer from a pay phone while taking a private bike ride to get the morning paper. There's no way he was going to stay for free, plus he believed in the curse and he wasn't going to take any chances with his family.

The anger in his voice could be heard from two feet beyond the pay phone booth. Mike Chitkowski insisted on paying for the vacation – after all it was the president who told him about the ETF's -affording him the money to purchase the condo in the first place. Second, he didn't need to worry about the curse, because the members of F.I.C were back in Connecticut with him. He will not accept any cash or check from the president – so don't be afraid of telling your wife and enjoy the island. (He hangs up on the president).

The ETFs purchased by Mike Chitkowski at $6.95 and $10.00 a share was currently selling for $29.90 and $37 a share according to the morning paper. "How can this be happening?" wondered Trevor Goodman. The treasurer must have sold all his shares and purchased the time share for around $8000.

At the East lighthouse, while walking down the cliff steps with his wife and kids, he decides to pull his wife aside to tell her what is going on. She can't believe what happened either and tells her husband everything will be all right. "Let's enjoy this week and send him a check in the mail as soon as we get back home."

The vacation week went by quick and the Block Island ferry was boarded by Trevor Goodman's family to return to Rhode Island. The weather, fishing, bicycle rides, beaches, restaurants, everything was perfect and he thought about owning a Block Island time share himself.

His cell phone rings just when they drove off the ferry onto the dock.

The call was from Jim O'Sullivan who informs the president that he is with Mario and Benny at the Foxwoods casino located just minutes from the Ct. / Rhode Island boarder. They want the president to join them for an unplanned F.I.C reunion.

"How did they know he was in Rhode Island?" asks Trevor Goodman.

Jim O'Sullivan called Gary's wife to look into renting the Block Island time share for his family and was told it was already booked by you. "In fact she called all of us to ask if we were interested in buying the time share for the third week in June... So, how about joining us at the casino?"

"I'm with my family, I can't leave them," answers the president. "Did Gary's wife tell you she recently sold the time share?"

"No," answers Jim O'Sullivan. "Did you buy it?"

The president tells him, "Mike Chitkowski bought it,"

"You're shitting me," exclaims Jim O'Sullivan, who tells Mario Bossi and Benny Benson the information.

Trevor Goodman's wife wants to know who the president is talking to on the phone. He tells her it's Jim O'Sullivan. "What going on?" asks the president's wife.

She' o.k. with him being dropped off at the casino, the kids and her can survive the ride home without him. "Are you sure?" asks her husband. "Positive," responds his wife. "I know you're dying to be with your F.I.C buddies, especially without Mike present, and it's been a while since you last saw them." (the president wishes his wife didn't use the phrase dying to be with them)

Mario Bossi, Benny Benson, Jim O'Sullivan, and Trevor Goodman meet at the race track section of the casino.

The waitress was told by Benny Benson to keep checking back to make sure there was always beer in front of the F.I.C members who now are betting on horses racing at Saratoga Downs.

A toast by Jim O'Sullivan included the fact that this was an unplanned F.I.C reunion, "to bad the treasurer couldn't make it."

"I forgot to call murderer," added Benny Benson while laughing out loud.

"He's going to be ticked off when he finds out about it," says Trevor Goodman.

"Who's going to tell him?" asks Benny Benson. Everyone pauses. He continues, "This is what he asked for, a F.I.C reunion without him, so he shouldn't be ticked off."

Jim O'Sullivan asks, "When did Gary's wife inform you of Mike buying the time share week?"

"She didn't," says the president. "The manager of the complex told me that I was staying for free, because the new owner had to pay the rental fee as part of the purchasing agreement. I'm going to send him a check as soon as I get back home."

"Why? He wanted you to stay rent free, so screw him," says Benny Benson.

"You know how he paid for the time share," asks Trevor Goodman? (Everyone is waiting for the answer.) "He used the profits from selling two ETF's I recommended while lying to him about owning the same stocks which have tripled in price."

"Unbelievable," answers Mario Bossi.

"Everybody look up at the board for Saratoga Downs – there's a horse named Bucket Head in the sixth race at 99 to 1," says Mario Bossi. "For the hell of it, let's bet $2 to show." Everybody places their bets on number two, Bucket Head.

With only four other horses in the race, Bucket Head seemed to be surprised when the gates quickly opened to start the race, but he starts to make a move just after the first turn. People are screaming and yelling Bucket Head's name has he builds up a two horse lead with about a quarter of a mile to go. Then, suddenly without any reason, Bucket Head moves away from the rail into the middle of the track, turns, travels head first towards the rail, and runs straight through the railing, killing the jockey and himself as pieces of railing go flying into the air. No body could believe their eyes. The body of the jockey was placed into the ambulance, and Bucket Head received a gun shot to the head in front of thousands of viewers.

The race track section of the casino was dead silent for a couple of minutes. The members of F.I.C and other gamblers in the race track are now quietly discussing the incident between themselves.

"No one is going to tell Mike about this reunion," demands Benny Benson.

"What did you just say?" asks Trevor Goodman.

"He can't find about the deaths of a horse and jockey we bet on. We have to promise each other that he never finds out, or he'll claim we are the Kiss of Death. This is an unofficial reunion, this doesn't count, because Trevor was never officially invited – he showed up unexpected."

"I wonder if this would have happened if I wasn't here," questioned Trevor Goodman. "Maybe I'm the curse."

"No way, it's him," says Benny Benson. Mario Bossi and Jim O'Sullivan are amazed Benny Benson is connecting the curse with the deaths of Bucket Head and the jockey.

"I think it's time to head home, whose capable of driving home?" asks Jim O'Sullivan.

The president says, "I'll drive home."

Everyone is sleeping and Trevor Goodman is doing all he can to stay awake when the traffic stops. He turns on the radio to a local station and hears there's an accident two exits down from were he is.

Benny Benson wakes up and asks the president what's going on.

"There's an accident up ahead of us, I'm going to get off the next exit," explains Trevor Goodman.

"I have to urinate," says Benny Benson as he starts to exit the car.

The president says, "Wait until we get off the highway."

"I can't wait." Benny is now urinating on the side of the highway as traffic starts to move again.

Just as Benny runs to catch up with the moving car, a state trooper pulls up with lights flashing.

The president had to leave the flow of traffic to move the car closer to Benny so he could safely reenter the car, blocking the right shoulder of the road.

The state trooper speaks through his car speaker to inform Trevor Goodman to drive the car back into traffic, so he can proceed forward to the accident.

"That was a close call," says the president." Next time I'm going to drive off and leave you on the side of the road."

"He knew I was taking a leak, they see it all the time"- responds Benny Benson.

Mario Bossi and Jim O'Sullivan wake up because of the noise from the trooper's speaker and they want to know why traffic is moving so slowly.

"There's an accident up ahead, I'm getting off at the next exit," says the president.

As they approach the accident scene, Life Star is landing on the same exit Trevor Goodman was planning on taking. "I guess were stuck in traffic again," laments the president.

"Good," says Mario Bossi; "I have to take a leak too," as he leaves the car to enter the woods, followed by Jim O'Sullivan.

With everyone back in side the car, the members of F.I.C are now close enough to see several cars involved with the accident. Two cars were so mangled, they looked like accordions.

Walking towards a state police car was a person wearing a trench coat and smoking a cigar while writing notes. Trevor Goodman couldn't believe his eyes – it was Detective Casella.

"I want you guys to look at the person in the trench coat walking towards the state police car. That's Detective Casella," points out the president.

"No shit." "He reminds me of some one," says Jim O'Sullivan.

"I wonder what he'd do if he recognized me driving by?" asks Trevor Goodman.

The car was within 10 ft. of Detective Casella and other troopers, when out of the blue, Benny Benson calls out the detective's name.

"What the hell is the matter with you?" asks the president. "This isn't funny."

The detective reacts to the calling of his name by looking towards the car, seeing Trevor Goodman in the driver's seat, and assumes he is the person calling for him. He tells the president to pull the car over behind a state police car.

"You're an asshole," says the president to Benny Benson, "Why did you have to open your freaking mouth?"

"I was just joking around, I didn't think he could hear me from this distance," says Benny Benson.

"How are you doing?"asks the detective. "Is there something I can help you with?" The detective couldn't understand why Trevor Goodman would call him way from the accident.

"Sorry to take you away from police business. Benny shouldn't have disturbed you by calling out your name." (The president looks at the person in the passenger seat while speaking to the detective)

"So you're Benny Benson," says the detective extending his hand, "Glad to meet you."

"When are you going to arrest Mike Chitkowski for murder?" asks Benny.

"If he's in the car, I can do it now," says the detective.

"He's not with us. This is Mario Bossi and Jim O'Sullivan," the introductions completed by the president.

The detective asks, "Where's Mike Chitkowski?"

"Unfortunately, he couldn't make the casino trip," says Benny.

"I need to get back to working the accident, however you saved me a phone call. Did the CFO and Susan pay the tap at the martini bar with cash or credit?"asks the detective.

"Cash," answers Mario Bossi. "Lots of cash. I couldn't believe my eyes, and so couldn't Mike Chitkowski when we saw the CFO with several hundred dollar bills in his money clip."

"Thanks. Niece meeting all of you." The detective returns to investigating the accident.

The passengers in the car are wondering the same thing, Why did the detective question the method of payment by the CFO and Susan? Why did Mario refer to Mike Chitkowski when confirming seeing large amounts of cash?

Is the detective piecing together information that could lead to further questioning of the members of F.I.C?

Trevor Goodman was able to drive his passengers safely home from the casino, but he wasn't going to get much sleep. The thought of the detective calling Mike Chitkowski was giving the president an anxiety attack.

"The check is in the mail, he should receive it by Friday of this week. I also included a note of appreciation," says Trevor's wife. "He'll send it back, but at least Mike knows we tried to reimburse him."

"Don't be alarmed, nothing happened to any F.I.C members, but I want you to look carefully at two pictures in this morning's paper." He shows his wife the picture of the car accident first, followed by the snap shot of a horse and jockey killed at Saratoga Downs race track. She only takes a second to view both pictures, and asks her husband,"Why am I looking at these specific pictures?"

He doesn't answer, but asks her to take a second look at both pictures. She takes an extra second or two and finishes looking at the pictures for the second time, and asks her husband, "What's going on?"

"I'm in the first picture. Look again at the person wearing a trench coat, standing talking to a driver of a car in the back round,. That's me talking to Detective Casella. The members of F.I.C bet on that horse to show because it was a 99 to 1 long shot just before it crashed into the rail."

She looks at the pictures for a third time. "You're not recognizable. How did you end up at the accident scene?"

"We were driving by when I told everybody that one of the cops investigating the accident was Detective Casella, and the next thing I know Benny is calling out his name. I end up introducing the members of F.I.C to him when he asks where Mike is. He also questions us about the CFO and Susan, asking us if they paid the tap at the martini bar with cash or credit."

"I wish you resigned as President of F.I.C a long time ago, this relationship you have with your F.I.C buddies is going to kill you. Do you think the CFO and the broker are criminals?"

"I don't know. I wish you didn't use he words "kill you" when speaking of F.I.C."

Today is the day the members of F.I.C. meet the members of B.S club. The 1pm. meeting on a hot summer Saturday after noon in Massschusetts, started promptly with Jack O'Brien introducing all the members. The B.S club members introduce each other, including their marriage status, and ages.

Since there were five members of F.I.C and only four members of B.S Club, the members of B.S Club were willing to retain the name of F.I.C, accept F.I.C's by-laws, pay dues set by F.I.C members, and keep the same F.I.C officers to make the merger happen.

Then Jack O'Brien said, "The firm wants to support its only investment club by offering to pay the dues for the clubs first month if you agree to merge."

They just went over board with that offer thought Mike Chitkowski. He knew who was behind the offer.

The members of F.I.C agree to merge with B.S, how could they not, everything was perfect.

On the way home from the meeting, Trevor Goodman, Jim O'Sullivan, and Mario Bossi, driving in one car, discussed the ease at which the members of B.S club made the merger happen.

"Call Benny first, and then Mike, see if they think the same thing," mentions the president.

Jim O'Sullivan calls Benny on his cell phone.

He agrees with everyone else, something isn't right; they made it to easy not to refuse. He concludes the phone call by telling Jim,"He's pulling into the firm's parking lot. He forgot his sunglasses at the meeting. Then he says to Jim,"To hold on, Mike's car is parked in a different spot from when we left the meeting, I wonder if he forgot something too? I'll call you back."

Benny calls right back, and notifies Jim he just left the building with his glasses and no one saw him enter or leave. This allowed him to walk to the back of the building were Mike's car was parked, to see if he was inside." You're going to think I'm making this up, but Mike and some other guy are talking."

The mastermind made one mistake. Jack O'Brien observed the exchange at the Olive Garden bar. In the process of kissing Jim Frond, a set of keys went from his hands into Susan's. The enhanced police photo of Mike's picture showed the set of keys in the photo matched the keys found in Susan's bloody pocket book at the accident scene.

A search warrant allowed Det. Casella to use the keys to enter the condo and open every door. In the basement, a small aluminum key opened an old four draw metal file cabinet. Forcefully pinching the release pins to remove the metal dividers, the Detective examined the first file – nothing unusual. He continued to remove the metal partitions to examine all the files when he saw the label (F.I.C) on the last one. He pulled out the file and read the information regarding F.I.C's association with the firm, again nothing unusual about the material. The Detective had to use a lot of force to reinsert the metal divider back into the draw, causing the pins to shatter and fly in the air. The open holes left by the missing pins exposed a white substance. The packets of drugs were concealed inside hidden compartments of the metal partitions separating file folders. The packets of drugs matched the ones found at the accident scene. All the packets were labeled with a red star stamped in the upper right hand corner. Every drawer that had metal dividers had crack cocaine hidden inside the partitions. The find would go down has the third largest crack seizure ever made in Massachusetts.

The detective calls the person who made the inquiry to update him about the search of the condo, and the location of files on F.I.C. The detective confirms the drug seizure and mentions his interest with viewing the surveillance tapes.

The money clip held several $100 dollar bills, confirmed Mike Chitkowski, plus he witnessed the CFO tipping the waitress $200. When told by the detective it was drug money, the stunned treasurer went speechless. In the conversation between the two men, nothing was mentioned about the chance meeting his F.I.C buddies had with the detective.

Mike Chitkowski told Trevor's wife he was sending the check back, and was glad they had a great vacation. The phone was passed over to the president and Mike explains to him that Detective Casella said the CFO and Susan used drug money to pay the bill at the martini bar.

"What else did he say?" asks Trevor Goodman.

"He said the drugs in the car matched the ones found in the condo."

"What else did he say?" asks the president

"He said the cause of the accident was a combination of speed (drugs) and alcohol, not murder."

"What else did he say?"asks Trevor Goodman.

"You've asked me the same question three times, and I know you well enough to know he forgot to tell me something important, so give it up."

"I did hear from Jack O'Brien, and all the paper work needed for the new investment club was completed."

"What did the detective forget to tell me?" demands Mike Chitkowski.

"It was an informal meeting, not a planned reunion. We crossed paths with the detective coming home from the casino."

"We, who's we?" asks the treasurer.

"Benny, Jim, Mario, and me, we traveled past an accident the detective was investigating when he saw us," answers the president.

"Another accident, only without me," interesting says Mike Chitkowski."

"There's no connection with us and the accident," responds Trevor Goodman."

"So no one died or was injured during your little secret get together without me?" asks Mike Chitkowski.

"Actually, there were two deaths at the casino, I mean at a race track where a jockey and horse were killed in a freak accident. This happened following Mario persuading all of us to bet on the long shot."

"Mario's the holder of the curse," exclaims the treasurer.

"I knew you would be happy to hear about a tragic story involving everyone else but you," says Trevor Goodman. Then adds, "No one connected to F.I.C died or was hurt."

"Still, you've got to admit something happened without me present," states Mike Chitkowski.

The president answers, "Yes, all of us felt the Kiss of Death Curse was in effect."

"Even Benny connected the curse with the deaths of the horse and jockey?" asks Mike Chitkowski.

"Yes, Benny tried to talk us into keeping it a secret because you weren't there."

"I can't wait to talk to him. I think I'll mention he's the curse and suggest the next reunion be held without him."

"Everyone is going to say it wasn't a planned reunion and no F.I.C members were killed."

"Was it a planned reunion or not?" asks the Treasurer.

"It wasn't."

"Still, something happened without me present, and everyone is connecting it to the curse, so I'm off the hook," says Mike Chitkowski.

"I guess your right." Should Trevor Goodman inform Mike about the knowledge of the secret meeting now or wait? He hates being president. This isn't going to be easy."Everyone knows about your secret meeting following the merger meeting, and your not going to be happy hearing Benny was the one who saw you."

"What are you talking about?"

"You know exactly what I'm referring to," answers the president.

"Damn, I can explain everything."

"You're going to explain it to everyone at my house, ASAP," demands Trevor Goodman.

"I'll be glad to get it off my chest. I just hope everyone will accept my apologies when they learn the truth," responds Mike Chitkowski. There goes the partnership.

The investigation by Det. Casella concluded with the arrest of Jim Frond, who had a saga of drug usage since his high school days. The brokerage firm was the perfect place to deal drugs, thought the master mind, but he didn't know one of his brokers was a trained uncover police officer.

Jack O'Brien's team installed the cameras and their efforts produced incriminating evidence that will hold up to any defense attorneys questioning – Jim Frond was history.

Jack O'Brien opened one of the metal dividers taken from the old cabinet recently removed by Jim Frond from his office, and along with Detective Rich Casella watched the gifted computer wiz's head drop as the sealed packets of crack cocaine and the packets taken from the accident were placed in front of Jim Frond for an explanation. The drugs in his system, plus the evidence placed in front of him, caused Jim Frond to sweat profusely with guilt.

Jack O'Brien and his team of officers (members of F.I.C II) receive commendations for their police work.

Mike Chitkowski is now the sole owner of "Strategies for Success" an online computerized program that every brokerage firm needs and wants.

Jack O'Brien asked Mike if he ever heard of a group of M.I.T. students who made millions of dollars beating the casinos in the game of blackjack, using a card counting system. No one knew about their secret until a casino investigator uncovered their system and notified casinos around the country to bar them entry.

"Yes," he's aware of the story.

Jack O'Brien uses the analogy to explain to Mike, the opposite is going to happen. "The entire investment world is going to open their doors to meet you. Diverse Investment's is lucky they have you as their new chief investment analyst. Congratulations!

PART 5

F.I.C II.

Jack O'Brien notifies his clients privately to sell General Electric after F.I.C II decides GE is going to be its first victim.

Five solid companies that generated billions of dollars worth of trading on the market, suddenly drop in value – what was happening questioned the experts.

Investors are starting to panic seeing the price of General Electric fall from $50 to $25 a share. The investment club purchases one hundred shares of GE at $25 a share. The stock rebounds within five weeks time to reach a price of $61 a share.

The whole country as well as foreign economists are confused by the markets sudden volatile swings and blame it on the anticipated rise in interest rates. Financial companies are not weathering the recent credit market upheaval and it's the end of September, investors who know the history of the stock market are worried about October.

What devastating force is causing investors to panic and sell their stocks? Why is it all happening now? Maybe it's the current exchange rate in Europe, were the U.S. dollar is worth less now then a few months ago. The everyday investor as well as the expert is wondering if another crash is imminent. Stock market speculation will always be an uncertain science claimed the experts – unless you're a member of F.I.C II.

The members of F.I.C II know what's happening, and their leader is becoming the world's greatest financial advisor that ever lived. Everything he predicted happened, and all of the world's online investors would love to have his system programmed into their computers.

Mike Chitkowski instructs F.I.C II to select Citigroup and UBS AG as their next victims.

Jack O'Brien is actually scared of a market crash and notifies clients to start to sell off their holdings, especially Citigroup or UBS AG.

Again, the investment club purchases large amounts of both stocks which quickly drop in price after each announces third quarter profit warnings. The companies also disclose the upcoming months don't look promising for maintaining normal earning levels. Citigroup drops from $47 a share to $28 a share. UBS AG drops from $54 a share to $34 a share.

In the past, F.I.C didn't reinvest profits, especially the first time they were successful in the market. Learning from the past, F.I.C II reinvests money, and purchases shares of Citigroup and UBS AG with profits made on GE, rather then visiting a race track or casino.

With a rocky October, November, and December, the market barely survives another crash, and then the Federal Reserve announces an unexpected interest rate cut for the end of the year, followed by banks and financial companies like Citigroup and UBS AG reporting normal earning levels have been maintained. The worst is over – they expect a positive four quarter.

The head lines in all of the major papers read, "Market Stages Huge Rally," the Dow Jones industrial average rises above 14,000 and well into record territory. The price of Citigroup and UBS AG rise to $57 and $63 a share. The members of F.I.C II have made more money in six months then they could have ever imagined.

Jack O'Brien's clients appreciated the warnings – but wondered why he never called previously to alert them. He knew before it was reported on CNN or in the Wall Street journal. How did he know prior to the rest of the world the stock market would tumble? His clients were intelligent investors; they needed answers – who alerted him?

Jack notifies his clients of a new online investment program that Diverse Investment's just developed, and will be available soon to the public at a cost. His clients want a guaranty at purchasing the program, no matter what the cost, before it goes public.

F.I.C II knows the recession has started, and is monitoring the response by the Federal Reserve board chairmen Ben Bernanke as to what the government is going to do to stop the economy from slowing dramatically. If the government only knew of F.I.C II and the powers they possessed, the Federal Reserve Board could quickly end the recession by eliminating the cause.

"I can't afford to be fit," screamed a long time member of Benny's fitness club, after informing Benny she received her notice indicating the increase in dues. Benny decided to raise the rates rather than lay off more personnel- a difficult decision.

The economy is causing the bottom to fall out of small businesses across the USA, and Benny wishes he sold the business three years ago to an interested buyer. The business as become a burden to heavy for his small shoulders to bear. Benny is starting to smoke and drink his way out of a major problem and the bills are pilling up.

The fitness club has been broken into recently for the third time and the police are investigating the theft as inside job. Benny has his first and only heart attack. The paramedics arrived within six minutes, but to no avail. Another F.I.C. member dies a tragic death.

The remaining members of F.I.C II are gathered at the funeral home, not knowing what to say to each other.

"I'm going to miss him," says a sarcastic Mike Chitkowski while holding his car keys in his hand. "About as long as it takes to get to my car."

"That's cold," remarks Mario Bossi.

"That's not funny, show a little more respect," counters Trevor Goodman.

"Actually, I think that was pretty good, coming from him," responds Jim O'Sullivan.

The members of F.I.C II say their good byes, and wonder which one of them is next.

The National Bureau of Economic Research (NBER), the organization that actually dates recessions, is interested in Mike Chitkowski's research, and is sending a member of its board to compare data with Mike.

"Don't panic. Wait one more week for the Fed's to react," suggests Mike Chitkowski. "The market is going to be very volatile for the next couple of weeks, possibly dropping several hundred points, before it rebounds upward."

The members of F.I.C II are trying to figure out what to do with their money. Should they listen to Mike or with their personal financial advisors who are suggesting other options?

Just as he predicted, the next week saw the market fall by three hundred points, and President Bush is now working with the Federal Reserve to create a stimulus package that will give U.S. citizens money in the form of rebates and tax credits. The package is designed to create spending, moving the market upward. Also, the Federal Reserve announced an emergency interest rate cut.

The Federal Reserve slashes its federal funds by 0.75 percentage points, to 3.5 percent, the largest cut since 1990. The market rebounds slightly with this announcement. The next Federal Reserve meeting is a week away, and every investor is wondering if another cut is coming.

According to Mike Chitkowski, they have to cut the interest rate at least another half a point to get investors happy again, and he thinks they will.

The opposite advice is being projected by Trevor Goodman's financial advisor, who warns the investor that even another rate cut won't be enough to steady the economy. He feels the Federal Reserve won't reduce the interest rate again, and a government bail out will take forever. Unfortunately, the advice last given to Trevor by his advisor was flawed. Should he believe him this time?

Jack O'Brien now wishes he remained a police officer. His clients are calling him 24 hours a day, wanting his expert advice. He contacts Mike and is told to wait a week for the Federal Reserve to announce another rate cut, before recommending the investors reshuffle their portfolios or buy discounted stocks. Jack passes the advice onto his clients, knowing in three months he would return to a career in law enforcement.

Who ever imagined Mike Chitkowski would be the person everyone trusts for advice concerning their money problems. When F.I.C started, he couldn't keep track of monthly dues never mind forecast the economy.

The confident innovator recommends the following actions; 1. Trust your instincts 2. Take advantage of discounted blue chip stocks and buy 3. Don't panic; don't reshuffle your portfolios until the Fed's reduce the interest rates again 4. Wait for the government to bail out the economy and relax, the recession has just started.

The formation of F.I.C. 21yrs ago in September of 1983, allowed the investment club to experience a market crash (87'), two recessions (91', 2001'), two wars (Desert Storm, Iraq),a terrorist attack(2001), a record closing high of the Dow Jones of Oct. 2007, and now a market upheaval of 2008. Amazing thought Trevor Goodman as he ponders what to do with his investment portfolio.

The confidence of Mike Chitkowski, his accomplishments, his accurate predictions, and his innovative program used by every brokerage firm that could afford purchasing it, yet his first words were "Trust your instincts."

If he goes with his instincts, Trevor Goodman will be the sole dissenter, creating a dilemma between the Treasurer and fellow F.I.C members. What kind of reaction will his F.I.C buddies have when the cautious President disagrees with the Treasurer's recommendations?

He calls Mario Bossi and Jim O'Sullivan, and explains why he's doesn't agree with Mike's advice. The government waited to late to act. He believes the country is in a recession, and the President's stimulus package along with more interest rate cuts, are temporary fixes that wouldn't be enough to end the recession. He's worried about another depression.

The other members question Trevor's decision, and remind the president of the final statement made by Mike. "As in the past, my opinions and predictions were accurate. At the end of the day, I don't think you're going to turn down my recommendations."

The Federal Reserve cuts the interest rates by another three quarters of a point, and the stock market rallies for the next couple of days. Mike Chitkowski, Jim O'Sullivan, and Mario Bossi call Trevor Goodman to rethink his position. The treasurer is the first to call.

"Have you changed your mind yet?" asks Mike Chitkowski.

"You say the recession has just started, and I respectfully disagree with you," responds Trevor Goodman. "Plus, I can't make payments on the Lamborghini I just bought. Should I ask the government to buy it for me?"

"What's gotten into you? Listen to me, the government is going to bail out the economy, I'm sure of it."

"The economy isn't the stock market, and my gut is warning me to go against the government, which means going against you!"

"I'm sorry that you feel that way, but don't come crying to me or your other friends when the economy starts to settle because of the government's involvement."

"Are you upset with my decision?" asks the president.

"Yes I am," answers the treasurer. "I've never let you down before, why would I do it now?"

"You're asking me to sit back and watch my money go down the drain while I wait for the government to bail me out. I don't think that's an acceptable solution."

"Millions of people across this nation are losing money, not just you. You say the government is late to act, but you're doing the same thing by moving your money into different areas. Why did you have your money in high risk funds to begin with? Why are you trying to correct the problem now, when you should have done it sooner? You're just like the government, but you don't agree with the government bailing you out."

"I'm not going to take as long as the government is to fix the problem. Look, I'm sorry, but I've made the decision to go with my instincts instead of yours. I am going to reshuffle 50% of my portfolio into cash. I never needed the government to bail me out before, and I'm not going to give in now."

"You're making a big mistake, the market and economy will recover sooner than you think. You need to rethink your decision before you act. History shows the market will rally over the next six months back to its normal level, ending the recession."

Just as the expert predicted, the Feds are doing everything possible to turn the economy around.

Treasury Secretary Hank Donley announces a 30 day pause for homeowners threaten with fore closers. This will give borrowers valuable time to work out refinancing terms with their lenders. Also, the Federal Reserve auctioned $30 billion in funds to commercial banks at an interest rate of 3% to promote cash-strapped banks with extra reserves.

A conference call was placed between Jim O'Sullivan, Mario Bossi, and Trevor Goodman. They tell him he's a jerk.

This is getting personal thought the president, but why?

The conversation starts with Jim O'Sullivan asking Trevor Goodman why he's rejecting the advice of Mike Chitkowski, causing friction between friends.

"Actually, I'm following my instincts as Mike recommended," answers a confident president.

"After six years of free expert advice, all of which was accurate, and financially rewarding for us, you're going to reject his recommendations without thinking about the consequences," remarks Mario Bossi.

Trevor Goodman asks Mario, "Consequences, what to you mean?"

"You know exactly what I mean," answers Mario Bossi.

"I'm afraid I don't," questions the president.

"By you refusing Mike's advice, we have to decide between you and him," explains Mario Bossi.

"No you don't. Just relax and follow your instincts, the recession has just started," says Trevor Goodman.

"Are you sarcastically making fun of Mike?" questions Jim O'Sullivan

"No. Just do whatever you both feel is right," suggests Trevor Goodman.

"Because of you, we don't know what's right. In the past, whatever Mike said to do was right, and we all supported his expertise. Now you're screwing everything up by saying he's wrong and your right." Jim O'Sullivan is trying to understand the president's view.

"That's not what I'm saying. I might be wrong too," admits Trevor Goodman.

"If your wrong and he's wrong, then we're in serious trouble, because we always trusted both of you,' says Jim O'Sullivan.

"Just trust your instincts," repeats the president.

"If you say that phrase one more time I'm going to kill you," threatens Jim O'Sullivan.

"Call your personal financial advisors to see what they recommend," suggests Trevor Goodman.

"That's the other problem; we don't have personal advisors, because they both died years ago. We used you and Mike for investment advice. We're asking you to reconsider your choice and follow Mike's advice, so that everyone can remain friends," begs Mario Bossi.

Trevor Goodman asks, "What's friendship got to do with making individual decisions concerning finances?"

"Because we never made any individual decisions regarding personal finances," acknowledges Mario Bossi.

"You're telling me you never replaced them with other advisors?" questions the president.

"We didn't need to, we had Mike giving us expert advice, and now you're pulling this crap, and everyone's upset," says a disgruntled Mario Bossi.

"Sorry, I never thought my decision would cause such turmoil between friends. I think both of you should follow his advice, "remember he's the expert.""

Jim O'Sullivan asks, "Why are you following the advice of your financial advisor over Mike's?"

"Are we in a recession or not? That's the question I asked him. He couldn't answer the question. Although he mentioned history shows a market decline often begins before a recession, it's hard for even experts to identify economic conditions admitted my advisor. He recommended the opposite advice of the treasurer. I disagree with my advisor's plan, but my instincts point towards the facts, even experts can't determine economic conditions."

"What a moron, now you're an expert all of a sudden," wisecracks Jim O'Sullivan. "I guess Mario and I have to choose between two experts. This isn't easy for us, because Mike wants to know what we are going to do."

"I told him what I'm planning on doing, and he'll get over it," assures the president.

"I don't think so," states Mario Bossi.

"I know he won't," exclaims Jim O'Sullivan.

"Let me know what both of you decide," asks Trevor Goodman.

They call two days after to confirm their support for Mike's plan, adding his predictions continue to be correct. Although, they do agree with him, the recession has started. They want to know why he's so stubborn. Just admit he's right and you're wrong, you don't know shit, and we're not waiting much longer for you to apologize to the Treasurer or you'll be down three friends.

Within the next three months, the Feds announce the checks will be in the hands of every U.S. citizen by May 1st. The reaction to the quickness of the Fed's stimulus package starts the market to move upward.

An e- mail from Jim O'Sullivan reads, "You're an Idiot". A second e-mail arrives from Mario Bossi, "stupid".

No correspondence from Mike Chitkowski.

Another four months go by, and the Fed's announce the possibility of reducing the interest rates again, predicting the recession will be over soon according to all economic indicators. This announcement excites the economy, and investors start to return to high risk stocks, such as small and large cap funds.

Examining his portfolio, if he didn't choose to reshuffle his assets into cash immediately, a profit of $2000 would have been accomplished.

More E-mails arrive from Jim and Mario.

"How's the expert doing now?" In spite of you're poor judgments, we realize that jealousy between friends occurs now and then."

A phone call to Mike Chitkowski allowed Trevor Goodman to congratulate him on his expertise.

"I appreciate the call, but wished you had listened to me. I'm leaving for Washington today to meet with the head of the NBER organization to compare notes. I'll call you when I return."

A conference call to Jim and Mario by Trevor Goodman warns his ex- friends that the big event is about to happen, but you two can't see beyond the right and wrong issue. The curse of all curses, a depression, is coming and the Fed's won't be able to stop it. The government is running a deficit now, releasing more money into the economy without reducing spending.

"Oh really," a surprised Jim O'Sullivan says. "That's it, we're never talking to you again, and we're going to inform Mike that he's no expert, but a person who can't be trusted according to the president, even though everything he predicted is happening."

"Yeah, and another thing, your not making any sense, even I know the government wastes money on pork barrel projects and over spends, but a depression can't happen in these modern times unless assholes like you start losing your jobs. Plus, we're in an erection year, and the new President of the United States will not let that happen," adds Jim O'Sullivan.

"I've told you a hundred times, using the word erection instead of election is not funny," responds Trevor Goodman.

Jim says, "That depends on who you say it to. Listen we're sick of hearing horrible stories about a depression, your making me depressed just listening to you talk."

"I believe the recession started when F.I.C II reentered the stock market. History of the investment club and the economy (stock market) co-exists, but this time the curse will last a long time, and so will the recession. Mike was correct long ago, we have a unique relationship that curses the stock market and now he's messing with the economy, need I say more."

"What you're trying to do is put the blame on Mike if a depression happens."

"That's nonsense," says Trevor Goodman.

"You get the blame if it happens. Maybe you're the holder of the curse and not Mike," questions the electrician.

The expert e - mails Jim and Mario to remind them to use his computer program to select stocks under the "safe" bar and then hit "in a pickle" site, producing names of companies affected by the economy. They purchase 100 shares of Barnes Group, a thriving aerospace company from the "safe list." Trevor Goodman never receives a call.

The president of F.I.C places more money into ultra safe Treasury bills after reading the Washington Post and large insurance companies across the United States are laying off 50% of their staff.

The NBER meeting ended and Mike needs to meet with Jim and Mario ASAP. However, he must talk to Trevor first. Mike e- mails Trevor Goodman."You were right, I was wrong. The country is in a recession. I have new data that shows you're correct. The recession is going to last longer than any of us experts could imagine. I hate to admit it, but pending the length of the recession period, a depression could happen."

Barnes Group reports its fourth quarter earnings were up 37% during poor economic conditions.

A conference call to Jim and Mario by Trevor Goodman, "Did you get an e- mail from Mike lately?"

"Yes we did, you probably ignored his advice again, and didn't look at the safe list. We bought 100 shares of Barnes Group," answers Mario Bossi.

"What did you do?" questions the president of F.I.C

"You know what, forget about Mike and us, you just do your thing. Don't act surprised when we trust our instincts and follow Mike's advice. The online program was given to you as a gift and you shove it up Mike's ass as if you could have afforded it on your own," says a ticked off Jim O'Sullivan.

"Yeah, this is your thank you but I don't need your program attitude. Go screw yourself!" exclaims Mario Bossi.

'What the hell are you two talking about?" questions the president again.

"We don't want to discuss your reverse relationship with Mike, because we're loyal friends. You're jealous of him winning over our friendship, because we agreed with him and you can't handle it," revealed Mario Bossi.

"I'm confused, the e-mail I received said I was right, and he was wrong. I never saw any e-mail relating to whatever you two are talking about."

"That's it; don't even think about calling us again. Your sick, get some help with your depression anxiety," recommends Mario Bossi.

Barnes Group reports next months quarterly statement will show a slight decrease in assets due to fewer military contracts.

On the plane, Mich Chitkowski reads the reports over and over again. How could he fail to connect the dots? Why doesn't he feel the need to stop the NBER from issuing a press release stating the recession is happening now. Economic history shows the event will last for only six more months. All he needs to do is call them back, and stop the release. Why is he afraid to do it?

After further reading, the data indicates the opposite, Why didn't anyone see the facts and connect the information to the current state of affairs? How did he miss interpret the facts? Would they listen to him and stop the release based on one person's view, without going through the whole process of meeting again?

He's thinking about Trevor Goodman, the curse (depression), and what to do as he claims his baggage at the terminal.

The woman was in her forties, in great shape, and decides to hold onto her purse while her attacker is dragging her through the terminal out the doorway into the street. Mich is calling 911 when her attacker releases the purse and drives off in a blue Mustang, leaving the injured woman lying on the sidewalk. He stays at her side until security arrives, gives the airport security the license number, description of the attacker, and then proceeds to his car, driving out of the parking garage in the direction of the assailant.

As Mike Chitkowski makes a turn around the exit to head towards I-91 South, a Mustang with shreaded front tires, traveling on its rims at a high rate of speed, followed by two state troopers in their vehicles, starts to crash into cars as the driver tries to elude police.

With in seconds, the life of Mike Chitkowski was taken by the head on crash, because he had no where to turn. The accidental death occurred on his 55th birthday: Feb 29th, 2008.

At Mike's funeral, Trevor Goodman felt a strange feeling deep inside his gut as he watches Mike's son approach the pulpit. Would the emotional eulogy include praising his father's efforts to save a marriage? Will Mike's son mention his father attempted the difficult task with assistance from the Goodman family?

Trevor Goodman's stomach was in complete paralysis.

Relief, not in the form of medication, but due to a shorten eulogy. Mike's son finishes his tribute to his father by revealing the treasurer felt being born on Feb 29th was a curse. "I guess he was right," sadly stated by a grieving son. Mich's son continued, "Many of his classmates in school would tease him about picking Feb 28th or March1st to celebrate his birth. This created a certain attitude towards celebrating family birthdays. Imagine living with a curse for your entire life."

The dazed members of F.I.C and their wives immediately look at Trevor Goodman as if he knew about the open secret. Like all the other onlookers, he's in shock.

Outside the funeral home parking lot, Mike Chitkowski's son approaches the F.I.C members carrying a small Igloo cooler filled with ice beer.

"My dad willed two gifts for each of you. First, a couple of ice beers to be downed with pleasure and memories, second, he wanted each of you to have whatever is inside these envelopes." Each envelope had the names of the remaining F.I.C members on them and a $6000 check inside. The note read, "I've made a lot of money because of you guys – enjoy some of it?"

The beer tasted good, even though many of the mourners thought it was inappropriate for beer to be consumed in a funeral parking lot and voiced their displeasure as they passed by.

Finishing his beer, Jim O'Sullivan looks at his wife and says, "I'm taking you to Italy,your wish has come true!" His wife gives him a huge hug and kiss.

"I guess you should fulfill your dream of flying with Jake over the Grand Canyon," adds Mario Bossi's wife. He gives his wife a huge hug and kiss.

"Whose Jake?"asks Trevor Goodman and Jim O'Sullivan at the same time.

"He's a Vietnam buddy who runs a helicopter service at the Grand Canyon," answers Mario's wife.

"What are you going to do with your gift?" asks Mario.

"I know exactly what he's going to do. He'll put the cash into some kind of safe money market account for emergency reasons, just in case the God damn depression happens," says an unhappy wife.

"I don't have to worry about a depression anymore, the curse as ended. The investigation is over, I knew right from the beginning he held the curse," concedes Trevor Goodman.

"If a depression happens, then he passed it on to you," remarks Jim O'Sullivan.

"No way, spend the money on anything you want honey, the curse has ended," concludes Trevor Goodman as he's hugged and kissed by his wife who screams about getting a new car.

Jim O'Sullivan mentions the stimulus package provided by the treasurer works better than the Governments.

Several months after the death of the treasurer, the Barnes Group announces a severe drop in earnings for the upcoming quarter.

CEO's from three blue chip companies suddenly resign from their positions, due to the announcement of massive layoffs within their companies.

The stock market nearly crashes.

The price of gas, predicted to reach $4 a gallon this summer, hits the mark in late March.

Syria is threatening Israel, and the U.S. is sending air craft carriers to the Middle East as a sign of support for Israel.

.U.S. investors are looking at investing in foreign markets, but the economies of foreign developed countries are declining as fast as the U.S. economy.

Within a month's time, Jim and Mario contact Trevor Goodman. How's everything going, still worried about a depression?

The president of F.I.C answers "Let me start by telling you my wife still hasn't bought a new car. Unfortunately, I'm scared of a depression and put most of my money into cash".

"We're still going to Italy in July, confirms Jim O'Sullivan. The trip has already been booked and nothing is going to stop us."

"Jake can't wait for us to arrive in Flagstaff, where he has a condo we'll use for free. There's no stopping me from flying over that canyon," proclaims Mario Bossi.

"I'm lucky to have all three jobs in town and plan on using my bicycle to get to work. I'll save a lot of money on gas, which we'll need for my wife's car."

"We want you to know we lost money selling the Barnes Group," says Jim O'Sullivan.

"I'm sorry to hear that, but why would I need to know?" asks Trevor Goodman.

"Because you predicted Mike carried the curse and didn't agree with Mike to purchase any stock from the "safe list" like we did. You were right and he was wrong," admits Mike Bossi. The president of F.I.C asks "I 'm not using his program anymore, are you guys?"

"No, we can't use it without his help, plus the "safe list" listed stocks that are now in trouble," confirms Mike Bossi.

"I wonder why he never sent me the e-mail he sent you guys about purchasing the Barnes Group," questions Trevor Goodman.

"Because he knew you wouldn't agree with him and we would," answers Jim O'Sullivan.

"I guess you're right," answers Trevor Goodman.

"So, tell us when you predict the depression is going to happen?" asks Mario Bossi.

"Tomorrow," joked Trevor Goodman. "I told you before, if the experts don't know, I certainly don't."

"We want you to make a prediction, just like Mike did," demands Mario Bossi.

"The probability of a depression will occur within a year."

"Seriously, make a prediction," requests Jim O'Sullivan.

"I just did. "I'll go on record and amuse you two jerks by saying within a year's time. How does October 9th, 2012 sound?"asks Trevor Goodman.

"Sounds good, if you are right, then the curse has been passed onto you," says Jim O'Sullivan.

"Gee, thanks a lot, but the curse as ended, remember that," Trevor Goodman responds.

"We'll see," answers Mario Bossi.

The next day, in the business section of the local paper, two pages are devoted to the question – Could a depression happen again?

Trevor Goodman as well as other readers, analyzing the facts and dates presented in the report, which listed in chronological order all the major economic events leading up to the great Depression and the present state of the economy, concluded another depression is possible.

At the conclusion of the report, one economic expert is quoted, "The economy is the top concern for voters and of keen interest to presidential contenders Senator Barak Obama and John McCain, who are gearing up for their party's convention. The upcoming election could follow financial storms brewing in September and October. If the newly elected President's economic plan fails, based on past historic dates, a complete collapse of the economy is predicted to occur in early October, 2012.

The remaining members of F.I.C are stunned, the curse continues, and the experts are confirming it.

PART 6

THE CURSE CONTINUES

Free lodging in Jake's condo, plus a complimentary dinner in Sedona with Jake, followed by practice flights and sightseeing, all included in the seven day vacation. However, the excitement of flying in a helicopter with his incompetent co-pilot created pressure, causing a migraine headache.

The first day of travel included a visit to the Grand Canyon with his wife. They left the condo located in Flagstaff, drove north up through a canyon pass, and spent the day walking the edge of the canyon. It was breathtaking, standing together on a sunny 55 degree October day, viewing this natural masterpiece created by Mother Nature. Suddenly, over their heads, the sounds of a helicopter flying at tree top level, just like in Vietnam, roars above them, disappearing into the depths of the canyon walls.

It brought chills to his body and scared the hell out of his wife, who didn't understand how helicopters were allowed to fly over people standing so close to the edge without any warning. He would learn later in the day that Jake would constantly ignore safety regulations and fly at restricted attitudes, especially since this was his last week of flying canyon trips – his mandatory retirement would become official on Friday of this week.

The meeting was scheduled for late after noon, which was perfect for the couple who wanted a full day at the canyon before they stopped to see Jake's heliport. As they drove into the crowded parking lot, a red and white colored helicopter, very similar to the one that flew over their heads hours ago, was parked on a cement pad with three other helicopters.

Upon entering the main lobby of the heliport, they notice large pictures of pilots flying canyon trips hanging on the wall. Jake, the most experienced pilot and part owner of the business, was pictured first. Jake's picture caught their attention, obviously taken years ago in Vietnam, a young man with medals pinned to his uniform.

A line of tourists are at the counter trying to arrange a flight with the ex-Vietnam pilot, who rumors say, thrilled his passengers with breath taking maneuvers around Mount Hayden. A person behind the front counter announces to all of the tourists, flights with pilot Jake Anderson are booked for the entire week. The only opportunity they have of flying with Jake is if someone cancels. Please include your names on the cancel list or book with other pilots for the week, there's plenty of flights available.

Mario Bossi and his wife are searching for Jake's office and find the hall way leading to all pilot offices. A conversation in the back office between Jake and another person who seemed to disagree with Jake's version of flying in restricted air space could be over heard by the couple. The person warned Jake to abide by the rules or his license could be pulled before he retires on Friday.

According to eye witnesses on the ground and in the air, Jake flew over restricted air space and buzzed people rafting on the Colorado River. Jake's business partner, as instructed, called Jake's psychologist to inform him about Jake's behavior.

Jake comes out of the back room to greet his old friend and his wife by asking them if they enjoyed their first day in Arizona. They did. Good, because its time to fly down to Sedona for supper pending the weather conditions. One of Jake's assistants informs Jake the weather in Flagstaff is wintery, with three inches of heavy snow predicted. Welcome to October weather in Arizona, were its sunny at the canyon, wintery in Flagstaff, and summer in Scottsdale, greets Jake.

The decision was to drive rather then fly in a snow storm down to Flagstaff. This allowed time to talk about old times and Jake's plan for practice runs and flight times. Another migraine head ache was avoided when told of the flight cancellation to Sedona.

After a few drinks and more conversation at the condo, the trio decides to drive down to Sedona for supper. Mario Bossi excuses himself from the dinner table to use the restroom, leaving his wife alone with Jake. Jake asks, "Do you believe in fate?"

Yes, she did.

"Amazing how lucky one person can be," states Jake.

"What do you mean?" questions Mario's wife.

"Your husband, the professional gambler, won a lot of bets on luck, although he thought it was his intelligence. He's healthy, married a beautiful wife, and is here with you because of unique unforeseen circumstances, someone could say fate or luck was involved."

"Thanks to Mike Chitkowski's gift and your hospitality, I agree, destiny calls."

"He was the best pilot I ever flew with, but unfortunately for him, I was the worst co-pilot. I never thought I'd get a chance to fly with him again, but I feel lucky to have the opportunity to prove to him how good I've become, plus I want to win the bet of a life time."

Mario Bossi returns from the rest room as his wife tells Jake, "Someone flew over us around 3pm. near the north edge of the canyon, was that you in the red and white helicopter?"

'That was me," answered Jake. Did I scare you?"

Mario's wife answers, "Yes. Are you allowed to fly at such low altitudes?"

"No. Sometimes I feel like I'm back in Nam and perform maneuvers used in combat by a pilot I use to fly with, (looking at Mario) which gets me into trouble. However, it also brings in customers who want the ride of their lives."

"Please don't do any of those maneuvers with my husband," demands Mario's wife.

"Don't worry honey; he's not going to be in the driver's seat, I am."

Jake responds, "We're sharing the driver's seat. Remember, I bet you a hundred dollars that my skills as a pilot are now equal to yours. Your money isn't safe; you might actually lose a bet with me after all these years."

"If you were allowed to fly as we did in Nam, you would lose your license, so there's no way to show off your new skills," says a confident pilot.

"I'm retiring officially on Thursday night, so Friday might be a perfect day to lose my license, especially with you as my co-pilot, don't break your promise."

"You're kidding, please tell me your joking," asks Mario's wife.

Mario's cell phone rings. A call from Jim O'Sullivan informs him that Trevor Goodman was going in the hospital for minor surgery, following a colonoscopy, "they found brain cells in his ass." The exam showed possible abnormalities between his intestine and gall bladder.

"Tell him I always knew he was an asshole, and then wish him luck," adds Mario.

Jake confirms he is joking, the flight will be safe, and invites Mario's wife to join them for Friday's flight.

"I'll think about it," Mario's wife doesn't believe Jake.

In two hours, Mario Bossi will meet Jake at the heliport, and fly with his long time friend again for the first time in Arizona. A migraine headache is starting and he asks his wife for an aspirin while trying to eat breakfast.

"That's the third migraine you've had in two days. What are you worried about?" asks his wife

"My Life," answers Mario Bossi. Flying with Jake always gave me headaches."

"No ones forcing you to fly with Jake. Don't fly if it's not safe," requests his wife.

"I can fly that copter safely with my eyes shut and without any practice, but I made a bet, and I never renege, never" replies Mario.

"Don't let him fly. You're risking your life and scaring the shit out of me because of a one hundred dollar bet, that's stupid."

"That's why were here, Mike's gift and my bet with Jake, which has to happen before he retires. I'm not going to lose, plus losing the money isn't going to kill us, remember the money isn't mind, Bob is actually paying him if I lose," kids Mario Bossi.

"Why did I have to mention flying over the canyon with Jake? I wish I thought of something else to do with that money. Please don't offer him the controls on Friday, bequeath him the hundred dollars on Thursday, and let him retire as a winner," begs his wife.

"I sorry, but when I shake some ones hand to seal a bet, I don't renege."

The flights were spectacular, occurring on clear, crisp, sunny days, filled with visual sights his wife will never forget. Flying above, below, and around the canyon for a couple of days gave the guests a true sense of the sheer size of this natural wonder. Dropping down several thousand feet to the Colorado River, then quickly back up to circle Mount Hayden, just took your breath away. Mario was lucky to have a buddy like Jake to fulfill his dream.

Mario's wife was amazed at her husband's skills of flying a helicopter. She was afraid of heights, yet he flew the helicopter with gentle movements, almost as if you were not inside the machine, but soaring over the canyon like a bird. It was only when they safely landed, did it dawn on her what it would be like to fly with Jake.

She considered it necessary to call Jim O'Sullivan and ask him if her husband ever reneged on bets made with the members of F.I.C.

The answer was, he never lost any personal bets. However, when he pooled his Super Bowl money and lost as everyone else did to Mike Chitkowski, he was very upset, but paid him.

Jim O'Sullivan asks, "Did Mario lose a bet with Jake?"

"I'm trying to avoid him losing his life because of a bet he made with Jake. Jake frightens me to the point of asking my husband to lose a hundred dollar bet and not allow him to fly with Jake."

"He'll never renege on a bet, especially if he shook your hand. He expected everyone to pay him if there was a gentleman's agreement," acknowledged Jim O'Sullivan.

"I wish I never mentioned using Mike's money to vacation in Arizona," lamented Mario's wife.

The confused friend asks, "Jake hasn't flown the helicopter yet?"

Mario's wife answers, "No, my husband has been at the controls all week. Tomorrow is Jake's turn, a day after he officially retires, and I'm scared about the measures he might take to impress my husband. Jake would have no problem losing his license to win a hundred dollars by proving he is capable of flying a helicopter like my husband."

Looking at Jake's records, the psychologist reads about a similar episode that happened a year ago when Jake was contemplating changing careers, but didn't because of a Vietnam buddy who talked him out of it. His Vietnam buddy wanted to fly over the canyon with him at the controls, and said the chances of getting to Arizona next year looked promising. The advice taken, Jake decided to work his last year and calmed down enough to regain control over the voices in his head who kept telling him to quit flying before he kills himself.

An hour session with the psychologist assured the examiner that one of the voices heard was his Vietnam buddies voice.

The phone call to Jake by his psychologist was intentional; the doctor considered it necessary to hear Jake say he wasn't taking his medicine on schedule and regretfully suggested not flying with his buddy on Friday.

Jake's business partner was contacted by the psychologist to request he not allow Jake the use of a helicopter on Friday. Something happened in Vietnam that shocks Jake's brains into abnormality and I'm certain it deals with a dangerous mission involving his Vietnam buddy and an incompetent co-pilot. Those two people should never fly together again with Jake at the controls. This is the first time the psychologist has ever broken a client's privacy, but he fears the safety of people over rides client privilege.

The call to Mario and his wife by the business partner on Friday morning allowed the couple to hear the good news.

He's not allowing Jake the use of a helicopter per doctors orders.

The time is 11:59am, and the helicopter is warming up with Jake sitting in the pilot's seat, waiting for his buddy to finish business in the restroom. As the propellers rotated around, Jake checks all instrumentations, and sees Mario finally coming out of the heliport door. Why is Dan, Jake's business partner walking behind Mario towards the helicopter?

The two men open the passenger side door and Dan asks Jake to shut down the machine.

"Why?" asks Jake

"We need to talk inside, in won't take long," Dan assures Jake.

Jake knows the flight is in jeopardy, but hopes an agreement can be worked out.

Dan gives the key over to Mario.

Mario Bossi, his wife, Jake, and Dan are taking seats in the office, when Dan hands the telephone to Jake.

Jake hears the familiar voice of his psychologist on the other end and says hello. The psychologist congratulates Jake on retiring and then gets right to the point by asking Jake why he hasn't been taking his medication.

"I forgot," the same answer Jake always uses.

"You know the agreement we have with the company and yourself – no medication – no flying."

"Did Dan call you?" asks Jake.

"Yes, and I'm glad he did. You can't be at the controls, you're lucky they didn't fire you before Thursday."

Jake is giving Dan an angry stare, hangs up the phone, and storms out of the office.

The couple proceeds to catch up with Jake and Dan outside the heliport, next to Jake's parked helicopter, clearly hearing them argue about his medication and the voices in his head.

Jake turns to his Vietnam buddy and says: "because of you they think I'm crazy."

Dan responds by stating, "That's not fair, he's upset, and didn't mean any harm."

"Bull Shit!" Jake is now letting it all out, "The medicine never worked, what I need to do is prove to him I can fly a helicopter."

"Don't let him fly," begs Mario's wife.

The Vietnam War was just a memory, today is reality, he decides in a split second to give his troubled buddy a chance to prove his worth as a pilot. He hands the key to Jake and both men quickly enter the helicopter to experience something more important to them, then anyone else could imagine. Mario Bossi never reneges on a bet. He looks at Jake, then his wife, and says the unthinkable – "you're on."

"Let me have the key," demands Dan who is trying to stop both men from entering the helicopter.

Mario's wife is screaming, "Give him the hundred bucks, it's not worth your life," while helping Dan stop the two friends from flying.

Dan and Mario's wife could only watch as the two Vietnam buddies begin the flight of all flights.

The helicopter starts to lift and Mario can clearly see through the windshield, his wife's expression of grief on her face. The last time he saw "the look" was when he announced he was going back to Vietnam for a second tour. The kids were young and she didn't want to go trough the horrors of war again, but he came back alive.

Jake piloted the helicopter upward in a vertical ascend, then leaned the helicopter forward severely, flying dangerously close to the heliport's roof, causing a migraine headache inside the head of his copilot, and heart attacks for people on the ground, along with people in the heliport office who thought the roof was going to blow off.

This is the final straw. Mario's wife decides now would be a good time to pack, leave her husband in Flagstaff and head for home without him. She leaves the condo and drives to the Phoenix airport to catch an earlier flight. Her cell phone rings just as she is pulling into the airports car rental parking lot. She refuses to answer the call. The phone keeps ringing and ringing, until she picks it up to see the call is from Jim O'Sullivan and let's the call enter her voice mail.

A police helicopter is dispatched to intercept the imaginary military helicopter now being flown by Jake Anderson. The pilot of the police helicopter makes radio contact with Jake and suggests he fly back to the heliport immediately.

After eluding the police helicopter for about and half an hour, and satisfying his buddy that he mastered the art of flying Vietnam type attack maneuvers, he returned to the heliport to be officially arrested and booked.

She is unloading the rental car and about to enter the airport when she decides to listen to Jim O'Sullivan's message. "Your husbands cell phone is completely filled with messages have him call me back ASAP."

A second call comes in from Jim, "I have an update regarding the President's surgery, unfortunately, problems occurred during the recovery stage, call me ASAP"

A third call from her husband at the heliport, he begs "I'm alive and the police have arrested Jake. Please wait for me at the airport, and don't leave." She's trying to figure out what to do, when Jim leaves another message on her voice mail. She decides to check the message.

"The President lost all sexual functions and can't remember anything, because the surgeon removed an abscess connecting his gall bladder and intestine to the frontal area of his brain which controls memory and masturbation. Call back ASAP."

She doesn't even crack a smile; the message was so stupid, she's sorry she even checked it. She calls back and quickly before Jim O'Sullivan could follow up with another stupid thought, she tells him he's to late; she's on her way home without him. Today is a day she wants to forget, a total disaster- my life is in shambles because of his stupid decision. (She starts to cry)

Jim O'Sullivan listens to her voice and asks his wife to listen to the phone message. After listening to the complete call twice, she agrees with her husband, something terrible happened to Mario Bossi.

He explains to his wife how Mario's wife feared Jake at the controls. She repeated several times, that she wished she never mentioned using Mike's money to fly over the canyon with Jake – checking to see if Mario would renege on a bet. "I guess she couldn't stop him from flying – I'm going to try and call her again."

His call placed but never answered.

"I'm going to cancel the trip to Italy."

"What are you going to do?" questions her husband.

Jim's wife responds, "The curse still lives, Mike's money is tainted with bad luck and Mario's wife, like me, sensed the connection, but acted to late. We're not using his money to fly to Italy, and we can't afford the trip, so I'm cancelling it."

"To tell you the truth, I wasn't looking forward to traveling to Italy in the first place. I can't believe what's happening - I only hope he's injured and not dead."

As the couple sat by the phone in the kitchen, they could hear the T.V., and CNN's Wolf Blitzer's voice announcing tonight's top stories. "We 're covering two breaking stories, one from the Grand Canyon and the other from Kennedy airport, say tuned for updates following the break."

The husband and wife can't believe the national media is going to confirm the tragic accident involving a friend of theirs. Do they want to hear the details?

"First, the events unfolding at the airport, hundreds of passengers are stranded at Kennedy Airport due to the FAA grounding certain airlines for trying to bypass safety inspections. All flights to Europe on Northwest and Delta airlines have been cancelled for the next four months to check all C-180 airplanes, usually used for transatlantic flights."

They both look at each other – Italy in July? They booked the flight on Delta.

"The rescue mission occurring at the Grand Canyon is on schedule. Engineers at the dam hope to complete the project within the next twelve hours. We will now show you live shots from our news helicopter."

Jim O'Sullivan's wife shuts the T.V. Off. "We don't need to see the pictures."

Her husband agrees.

She immediately walks over to the computer room and turns on the computer. She brings up the site containing their Italy confirmation numbers, seat assignments, and hotel accommodations, and cancels everything.

I'm going to call Trevor Goodman and let him know what happened.

"I hope your sitting down - there's been a tragic accident involving Mario at the Grand Canyon near the dam. We couldn't watch the details on CNN, but his wife confirmed it over the phone."

Trevor asks, "When did it happen?"

"Yesterday – some time in the afternoon."

"I just watched the news on CNN, all they showed was the rescue attempt of the Colorado River, by releasing thousands of gallons of water at the dam. The picture from the helicopter was spectacular."

"They didn't show the accident, only water coming out of the dam!"

"That's right."

"What the hell is so news worthy about water coming out of a dam?"

"The engineers, by releasing water at the northern dam, can resupply the Colorado river with valued water. At the beginning of the river water is plentiful, but as it flows into the Gulf of California, it dries up, due to the lack of precipitation, and water demand. Engineers will perform rescue missions every ten years or so, pending the demand for water by all five states the river flows through."

"We thought the news was about rescuing Mario, not a river."

Trevor Goodman suggests they try to contact Mario's wife again to make sure they have the correct facts.

"We just cancelled our trip to Italy because of the connection between Mike's money and the death of Mario."

"He's dead, are you sure?"

"Jesus, I hope he's alright, she sounded as if he was dead or seriously injured."

Trevor Goodman gets through to Mario's wife, and asks about her husband's condition.

She explains the whole situation, and could see how it might have confused Jim, based on previous conversations. The fact of the matter is he's alive and well - she will call Jim to explain the whole misunderstanding as soon as they arrive in Connecticut.

Jim O'Sullivan and his wife, attempt to reschedule their Italy trip, but can't retain the same package. They decide to book a cruise to Italy instead, costing less then the original trip. Plus, the cruise will occur a week after Jim retires – a retirement gift.

A die hard Red Sox fan with six months remaining until retirement, he never imagined being assigned to New York City – the job site of the new Yankee Stadium - he's ticked off. He asks for a transfer to another job – rejected – his anger is directed at the new stadium.

The task shouldn't take longer than two hours to accomplish – can his cohorts be trusted?

Yes, because they hated the Yankees more then he did, and they believed in curses – like the curse of the Bambino.

He's going to miss the autographed shirt signed by his favorite player David Ortiz, but just like the player himself, who destroyed the Yankees with his bat, the master electrician will use his shirt to curse the new home of the Evil Empire. Just like the Kiss of Death Curse that devastated the stock market and the economy, the David Ortiz curse will reduce the Evil Empire's home to rubble – the shirt is buried beneath the floor cement on level two - section C.

Should Jim O'Sullivan inform his two F.I.C buddies, both Yankee fans, that he just gave himself the best retirement gift imaginable? Can they be trusted? Would they believe him? He decides to wait and see how the 2009 baseball season turns out for the Yankees.

T.V. stations out of Boston and New York report investigating a rumor of a David Ortiz uniform shirt buried in floor cement within Yankee Stadium– cursing the new home of the Bronx Bombers. A tip led the Yankee organization to the exact location of the buried shirt.

Jim O'Sullivan calls his cohorts, who reassure him; his name will never be known, explaining they were drunk when they misspoke. A drop dead gorgeous sports reporter happened to be in the bar when she tricks them into talking about the curse – in exchange for sex.

Trevor Goodman and Mario Bossi make the connection, David Ortiz was his favorite player, the person involved believed in the power of curses, they ask him to see the autographed uniform worn by David Ortiz displayed in his recreation room. He denies being involved. They know it's him and threaten to go public if he doesn't show them the shirt or confess. He confesses and both friends are furious - he placed a curse on their favorite team.

Directing the response to Jim, Trevor Goodman says, "Mike had the divine power to carry a curse and now you intentionally bring bad luck to the Yankees,"

"It was a retirement gift to me."

"We're going to call the papers to report the name of the individual responsible for the evil act – cursing you!" exclaims Mario Bossi.

"No your not. How would that curse me?"

"Did you do the dirty deed alone?"asks Trevor Good-man.

"No, two other co- workers helped."

Mario Bossi asks "Are you worried about them divulging your name?"

"No."

"They will and that will in turn curse you. What you did was terrible," added Mario Bossi.

"Relax, nobody got hurt. I understand the shirt is up for auction, with the proceeds going to the Jimmy Fund. My prank is benefiting someone - just like the Kiss of Death curse."

Trevor Goodman states, "If the Yankees start to win again, your name is safe. However, we will not hesitate to inform the media who was responsible for the down fall of the Yankees if they continue to lose."

Jim O'Sullivan answers, "Fair enough."

The members of F.I.C are stunned by the news of the Treasury asking for $700 billion to bail out the economy from entering a depression. It's the largest government bailout in U.S. history and the American people are going to foot the bill.

The Presidential debates are scheduled for the up coming week, what are McCain's and Obama's positions on the bail out? Who are they going to blame for the distressed economy? What's their plan to alleviate the nation's economic troubles?

Jim O'Sullivan and Mario Bossi want Trevor Goodman to predict what the presidential candidates will do.

The candidate that votes for the bailout will not be the next president, predicts the President of F.I.C.

And what if they both vote for it?

"They won't," says a confident President. He's sure McCain will vote no.

Both presidential candidates vote for the bailout.

The final presidential debate completed, the President of F.I.C knows who he'll vote for and so do the other members of F.I.C.

According to the polls, the economy is the number one issue of voters.

With twenty days left, the race is still close. Can the stock market manage through Nov. 4th without crashing?

What effect will the winner of the presidential race have on the market?

Most Americans hearing the breaking news on radio and T.V. thought the new President of the United States message was to announce the official start of the depression, since additional banks across the country are closing at alarming rates, and inflation is at record levels. Americans continue to lose their jobs and the stock market is close to crashing. It came as a shock to hear the President of the United States announce a nuclear attack on Iran.

The United States and Israel's intelligence agencies have confirmed the presence of two small nuclear warheads being transported through Syria, in an attempt to assist Iran with a nuclear attack on Israel and U.S. Troops withdrawing from Iraq. In a nationally televised speech, the new President of the United States shocks the world and Americans alike by announcing the destruction of Iran's nuclear warheads by Israel and U.S. nuclear weapons. The President acknowledges the Congress and Senate, in a secret meeting yesterday, decided time was urgent – intelligence determined the two nuclear attacks were planed for today, Sept. 10, 2012, the date considered by all Americans as the final day of victory in Iraq allowing the last brigade of U.S. troops to come home safely.

Bomb, bomb, bomb Iran, just what McCain joked about during the primaries.

Only countries associated with terrorism condemn the nuclear attack on Iran. The rest of the world is astonished to learn of the accuracy of the attack and how little collateral damage occurred. One bomb, no U.S. soldiers killed, enemy destroyed. The message sent – the U.S. will not hesitate to strike first to save the lives of U.S. soldiers and its citizens from terrorists attacks.

Many listeners, including the members of F.I.C, hear the President of the United States reference to the economy. "We can defend ourselves under extreme economic conditions. This country and its allies know retaliation by Iran is expected, but I assure the American people our defensive systems are at work as I speak. You are safe from any nuclear attacks." He continues, "The United States is and always will be the strongest military power in the world as long as I'm in charge. Starting tomorrow, allies of the United States have committed to secure the region in question, allowing the remaining brigades of U.S. soldiers to return home as planned. The world is watching and knows the people of the United States and their President will not be intimidated by terrorists seeking to kill Americans and their allies for the right to live under a free democracy. The United States wants a world full of peace and prosperity, we had no other option. I'm proud to be the President of the greatest country in the world, God bless America."

The Congress and the Senate agreed with the President of the United States, solidarity exists but it took a nuclear threat to bring all political parties together -amazing.

The curse of all curses, a depression, suddenly disappears. The stock market reopens, food centers start to turn back into supermarkets, banks reopen on a daily basis, gasoline prices start to drop because Turkey resupplies the U.S. with plenty of gasoline in exchange for intelligence provided by U.S. agencies regarding Iran's next target – Turkey. Jobs increase due to billions of dollars of foreign money sent to U.S. by Israel as a thank you for saving their asses, and finally, since the connection to the planned attack included Syria's help, the U.N. actually condemns Syrians leaders and seeks monetary retribution for its actions.

PART 7

THE FINAL DAYS

The weather was horrible; the first day at the convalescent home will keep the three amigos inside, no putting on the practice green behind the facility. The plan was to leave the practice green and sneak over to the OTB three blocks down the street. Then return for supper, sneak out to the local bar while the movie was playing to smoke their cigars while they chatted with the young big breasted bartenders.

The idea of living out their final years on earth in the same convalescent home was discussed a few times – but now its reality.

Since their families brought their grandfathers to the same doctors, churches, restaurants, senior centers, hospitals, and drug stores, they agreed to put the three stooges in the same home. The only concerns the families had was with the staff – can they handle the daily problems the three misfits were going to cause? The staff quickly put the three friends on notice.

This didn't stop them from: 1. Physically fighting with the other male residents 2. Drinking ice beer in restricted areas of the home, like the fitness area 3. Line up in front of the main elevator to question new female arrivals as to their wealth and married status while sitting in their wheelchairs holding onto their ice beers 4. Pulling all nighters with card games and porno flicks snuck into their rooms 5. Using the remote fart machine during Sunday Mass. 6. Teaching the talking parakeets in the cafeteria how to speak to the ladies – "Go back to the race track you old bitch" and when a man approached the bird cage – "What are you looking at you bald headed bastard" .6. Stealing other male resident's walkers or canes while they tried to pick up the attractive wealthy widower, allowing them to get to her first.

The families of the remaining F.I.C members noticed the breakdown of their Dads when the shenanigans' started to stop. They no longer had the energy to plan and execute their schemes.

Well into their eighties, the curse of age is harming them daily with strokes, seizures, and heart attacks.

Mike Chitkowski's predictions with the stock market, economy, and order of death of F.I.C members were inaccurate. The last member to die, Jim O'Sullivan, witnessed the President of F.I.C pass away with a smile on his face – he's last words were "I resign."

Following the President's death, Jim O'Sullivan purchased the last Power Ball ticket requested by Mario Bossi, and quickly calculated the winning ticket to be around 10 million after taxes. To bad he'll never see a penny. Luck finally ran out.

At ninety two, Jim O'Sullivan dies a millionaire, thanks to Mario's family and decides to donate a large portion of money for the establishment of F.I.C III, an investment club made up of sons and daughters of the seven original F.I.C members.